'Don't play games with me,' Erin urged, breathing in deep and slow, her nostrils flaring in dismay at the familiar spicy scent of his designer aftershave.

The smell of him, so achingly familiar, unleashed a tide of memories. But Cristo had not made a commitment to her, had not done anything to make her feel secure, and had never once mentioned love or the future. Her soft full mouth turned down at the recollection. At the end of the day, in spite of all her precautions, he had still walked away untouched while she had been crushed in the process.

She had had to accept that all along she had only been Miss All-Right-For-Now on his terms—not a woman he was likely to stay with, just one more in a long line.

Lynne Graham was born in Northern Ireland and has been a keen Mills & Boon® reader since her teens. She is very happily married, with an understanding husband who has learned to cook since she started to write! Her five children keep her on her toes. She has a very large dog, which knocks everything over, a very small terrier, which barks a lot, and two cats. When time allows, Lynne is a keen gardener.

Recent titles by the same author:

A VOW OF OBLIGATION
  (Marriage by Command)
DEAL AT THE ALTAR
  (Marriage by Command)
ROCCANTI'S MARRIAGE REVENGE
  (Marriage by Command)
JEWEL IN HIS CROWN

Did you know these are also available as eBooks?
Visit www.millsandboon.co.uk

THE SECRETS
SHE CARRIED

BY
LYNNE GRAHAM

MILLS & BOON

First published in Great Britain 2011
by Mills & Boon, an imprint of Harlequin (UK) Limited.
Harlequin (UK) Limited, Eton House, 18-24 Paradise Road,
Richmond, Surrey TW9 1SR

© Lynne Graham 2012

ISBN: 978 0 263 89086 0

Harlequin (UK) policy is to use papers that are natural, renewable and recyclable products and made from wood grown in sustainable for-ests. The logging and manufacturing process conform to the legal environmental regulations of the country of origin.

Printed and bound in Spain
by Blackprint CPI, Barcelona

THE SECRETS
SHE CARRIED

pied a category all of her own in his memories, for
she had been the only woman ever to betray him and,
even though almost three years had to have passed since
their last meeting, the recollection could still sting. His
keenly intelligent gaze devoured the photograph of his
former mistress standing smiling at the elbow of Sam
Morton, the elderly owner of Stanwick Hall. Clad in a
dark business suit with her eye-catching hair restrained
by a clip, she looked very different from the carefree,
casually clad young woman he remembered.

His tall, powerful body in the grip of sudden tension,
Cristo's dark-as-night eyes took on a fiery glow. That
fast he was remembering Erin's lithe form clad in silk
and satin. Even better did he recall the wonderfully slip-
pery *feel* of her glorious curves beneath his appreciative
hands. Perspiration dampened his strong upper lip and
he breathed in deep and slow, determined to master the
near instantaneous response at his groin. Regrettably,
he had never met another Erin, BUT then he had married soon afterwards and only in recent months had he
again enjoyed the freedom of being single. He knew that
a woman capable of matching his hunger and even of
occasionally exhausting his high-voltage libido was a
very rare find indeed. He reminded himself that it was
very probably that same hunger that had led her to betray his trust and take another man into her bed. An un-
apologetic workaholic, he had left her alone for weeks
while he was abroad on business and it was possible that
he had invited the sordid conclusion that had ultimately
finished their affair, he conceded grudgingly. Of course,
had she agreed to travel with him it would never have
happened but regrettably it had not occurred to him at

the time that she might have excellent, if nefarious, reasons for preferring to stay in London.

He studied Sam Morton, whose body language and expression were uniquely revealing to any acute observer. The older man, who had to be comfortably into his sixties, could not hide his proprietorial protective attitude towards the svelte little manager of his health spas. His feelings shone out of his proud smile and the supportive arm he had welded to her spine in a declaration of possession. Cristo swore vehemently in Greek and examined the photo from all angles, but could see no room for any more innocent interpretation: she was at it again…bedding the boss! While it might have done him good to recognise Erin's continuing cunning at making the most of her feminine assets, it gave him no satisfaction at all to acknowledge that she was still happily playing the same tricks and profiting from them. He wondered if she was stealing from Morton as well.

Cristo had dumped Erin from a height when she let him down but the punishment had failed to soothe an incredulous bitterness that only increased when he had afterwards discovered that she had been ripping him off. He had had faith in Erin, he had trusted her, had even at one point begun to toy with the idea that she might make a reasonable wife. Walking into that bedroom and finding another man in the bed he had planned to share with her, along with the debris of discarded wine glasses and the trail of clothes that told its own sleazy story, had knocked him sideways. And what had he done next?

Lean, strong face rigid, Cristo grudgingly acknowledged his own biggest mistake. In the aftermath of his discovery that Erin had cheated on him, he had reached a decision that he was still paying for in spades. He had made a wrong move with long-term repercussions and for a male who almost never made mistakes that remained a very humbling truth. With hindsight he knew exactly why he had done, what he had done but he had yet to forgive himself for that fatal misstep and the fallout those closest to him had suffered. Handsome mouth compressed into a tough line at that reflection, he studied Erin closely. She was still gorgeous and doubtless still happily engaged in confidently plotting and planning how best to feather her own nest while that poor sap at her elbow gave her his trust and worshipped the ground her dainty feet trod on.

But Cristo knew that he had the power to shift the very ground in an earthquake beneath those same feet because he very much doubted that the reputedly conservative and morally upright Sam Morton had any awareness of the freewheeling months that Erin had enjoyed in her guise as Cristo's mistress, or of the salient fact that at heart she was just a common little thief.

That bombshell had burst on Cristo only weeks after the end of their affair. An audit had found serious discrepancies in the books of the health spa Erin had been managing for him. Products worth a considerable amount of money had gone missing. Invoices had been falsified, freelance employees invented to receive pay cheques for non-existent work. Only Erin had had full access to that paperwork and a reliable long-term employee had admitted seeing her removing boxes of products from the store. Clearly on the take from the day that Cristo hired her, Erin had ripped off the spa to the tune of thousands of pounds. Why had he not prosecuted her for her thieving? He had been too proud to parade the reality that he had taken a thief to his bed and put a thief in a position of trust within his business.

Erin was a box of crafty tricks and no mistake, he acknowledged bitterly. No doubt Morton was equally unaware that his butter-wouldn't-melt-in-my-mouth employee played a very creditable game of strip poker. That she had once met Cristo at the airport on his birthday wearing nothing but her skin beneath her coat? And that even the coat had gone within seconds of entering his limousine? Did she cry out Morton's name and sob in his arms when she reached a climax? Seduce him as only a very sensual woman could while he tried to give the business news his attention instead? Most probably she did, for she had learned from Cristo exactly what a man liked.

Disturbed that he still cherished such strong memories of that period of his life, Cristo poured himself a whisky and regrouped, his shrewd brain swiftly cooling the tenor of his angry reflections. The phrase, 'Don't get mad, get even' might well adorn Cristo's gravestone, for he refused to waste time on anything that didn't enrich his life. So, Erin was still out there using her wits and her body to climb the career and fortune ladder. How was that news to him? And why was he assuming that Sam Morton was too naïve to know that he had caught a tiger by the tail? For many men the trade-off of as much sex as a man could handle would be acceptable.

And Cristo registered in some surprise at his predictability that he was no different from that self-serving libidinous majority. I could go there again, he thought fiercely, his adrenalin pumping at the prospect of that sexual challenge. I could really *enjoy* going there again. She's wasted on an old man and far too devious to be

contained by a male with a conventional outlook. He
began to read the file, discovering that Erin's wealthy
employer was a widower. He could only assume that
she had her ambition squarely centred on becoming
the second Mrs Morton. Why else would a scheming
gold-digger be working to ingratiate herself and earn a
fairly humble crust? He was convinced that she would
not have been able to resist the temptation of helping
herself to funds from Sam Morton's spas as well.

Her healthy survival instincts and enduring cunning
offended Cristo's sense of justice. Had he really believed
that such a cool little schemer might turn over a new leaf
in the aftermath of their affair? Had he ever been that
naïve? Certainly, he had compared every woman he had
ever had in his bed to Erin and found them all wanting
in one way or another. That was a most disconcerting
truth to accept. Clearly, he had never got her out of his
system, he reflected grimly. Like a piece of baggage he
couldn't shed, she had travelled on with him even when
he believed that he was free of her malign influence.
It was time that he finally stowed that excess baggage
and moved on and how better to do that than by exorcis-
ing her from his psyche with one last sexual escapade?

He knew what Erin Turner was and he also knew that
memory always lied. Memory would have embellished
her image and polished her up to a degree that would
not withstand the harsh light of reality. He needed to
puncture the myth, explode the persistent fantasy and
seeing her again in the flesh would accomplish that de-
sirable conclusion most effectively. A hard smile slashed
Cristo's handsome mouth as he imagined her dismay at
his untimely reappearance in her life.

'Look before you leap,' his risk-adverse foster mother

had earnestly told him when he was a child, fearing his adventurous, rebellious nature and unable to comprehend the unimaginably entertaining attraction of taking a leap into the unknown. In spite of all his foster parents' efforts to tame his passionate temperament, however, Cristo's notoriously hot-blooded Donakis genes still ran true to form in his veins. His birth parents might not have survived to raise their son but he had inherited their volatile spirits in the cradle.

Without a second thought about the likelihood of consequences, indeed merely reacting to the insidious arousal and sense of challenge tugging at his every physical sense, Cristo lifted the phone. He informed the executive head of his acquisitions team that he would be taking over the next phase of the negotiations with the owner of the Stanwick Hall Hotel group.

'Well, what do you think?' Sam prompted, taken aback by Erin's unusual silence by his side. 'You needed a new car and here it is!'

Erin was still staring with a dropped jaw at the top-of-the-range silver BMW parked outside the garages for her examination. 'It's beautiful but—'

'But *nothing*!' Sam interrupted impatiently as if he had been awaiting an adverse comment and was keen to stifle it. Only marginally taller than Erin's five feet two inches, he was a trim man with a shock of white hair and bright blue eyes that burned with restive energy in his suntanned face. 'You do a big important job here at Stanwick and you need a car that suits the part—'

'Only not such an exclusive luxury model,' she protested awkwardly, wondering what on earth her colleagues would think if they saw her pulling up in a vehicle that undoubtedly cost more than she could earn in several years of employment. 'That's too much—'

'Only the best for my star employee,' Sam countered with cheerful unconcern. 'You're the one who taught me the importance of image in business and an economical runabout certainly doesn't cut the mustard.'

'I just can't accept it, Sam,' Erin told him uncomfortably.

'You don't have a choice,' her boss responded with immoveable good humour as he pressed a set of car keys into her reluctant hand. 'Your old Fiesta is gone. Thanks, Sam, is all you need to say.'

Erin grimaced down at the keys. 'Thanks, Sam, but it's too much—'

'Nothing's too good for you. Take a look at the balance sheets for the spas since you took over,' Sam advised her drily. 'Even according to that misery of an accountant I employ I'm coining it hand over fist. You're worth ten times what that car cost me, so let's hear no more about it.'

'Sam…' Erin sighed heavily and he filched the keys back from her to stride over to the BMW and unlock it with a flourish.

'Come on,' he urged. 'Take me for a test drive. I've got some time to kill before my big appointment this afternoon.'

'What big appointment?' she queried, shooting the sleek car into reverse and filtering it out through the arched entrance to the courtyard and down the drive past the immaculate gardens.

'I'm having another bash at the retirement thing,' her boss confided ruefully.

Erin suppressed a weary sigh. Sam Morton was al-

ways talking about selling his three country-house hotels, but she believed that it was more an idea that he
toyed with from time to time than an actual plan likely
to reach fruition. At sixty-two years of age, Sam still
put in very long hours of work. He was widowed more
than twenty years earlier and childless; his thriving hotel
group had become his life, consuming all his energy
and time.

Thirty minutes later, having dropped Sam off at his
golf club for lunch and gently refused his offer to join
him in favour of getting back to work, Erin walked back
into Stanwick Hall and entered the office of Sam's secretary, Janice, a dark-haired fashionably clad woman
in her forties.

'Have you seen the car?' she asked Janice with a self-
conscious wince.

'I went with him to the showroom to choose it—
didn't I do you proud?' the brunette teased.

'Didn't you try to dissuade him from buying such an
expensive model?' Erin asked in surprise.

'Right now, Sam's flush with the last quarter's profits
and keen to splurge. Buying you a new car was a good
excuse. I didn't waste my breath trying to argue with
him. When Sam makes up his mind about something
it's set in stone. Look at it as a bonus for all the new clients you've brought in since you reorganised the spas,'
Janice advised her. 'Anyway you must've noticed that
Sam is all over the place at the moment.'

Erin fell still by the other woman's desk with a frown.
'What do you mean?'

'His moods are unpredictable and he's very restless.
I honestly think that he's really intending to go for re-

tirement this time around and sell but it's a challenge
for him to face up to it.'

Erin was stunned by that opinion for she had learned
not to take Sam's talk of selling up seriously. Several
potential buyers had come and gone unmourned during
the two years she had worked at Stanwick Hall. Sam
was always willing to discuss the possibility but had yet
to go beyond that. 'You really think that? My word, are
half of us likely to be standing in the dole queue this
time next month?'

'Now that's a worry I *can* settle for you. The law
safeguards employment for the staff in any change of
ownership. I know that thanks to Sam checking it out,'
Janice told her. 'As far as I know this is the first time
he's gone that far through the process before.'

A slight figure in a dark brown trouser suit, silvery
blonde hair gleaming at her nape in the sunlight, Erin
sank heavily down into the chair by the window, equal
amounts of relief and disbelief warring inside her, for
experience had taught her never to take anything for
granted. 'I honestly had no idea he was seriously considering selling this time.'

'Sam's sixtieth birthday hit him hard. He says he's
at a turning point in his life. He's got his health and his
wealth and now he wants the leisure to enjoy them,'
Janice told her evenly. 'I can see where he's coming
from. His whole life has revolved round this place for
as long as I can remember.'

'Apart from the occasional game of golf, he has nothing else to occupy him,' Erin conceded ruefully.

'Watch your step, Erin. He's very fond of you,' Janice
murmured, watching the younger woman very closely
for her reaction. 'I always assumed that Sam looked

on you as the daughter he never had but recently I've begun to wonder if his interest in you is quite so squeaky clean.'

Erin was discomfited by that frankly offered opinion from a woman whom she respected. She gazed steadily back at her and then suddenly helpless laughter was bubbling up in her throat. 'Janice…I just can't even begin to imagine Sam making a pass at me!'

'Listen to me,' the brunette urged impatiently. 'You're a beautiful woman and beautiful women rarely inspire purely platonic feelings in men. Sam's a lonely man and you're a good listener and a hard worker. He likes you and admires the way you've contrived to rebuild your life. Who's to say that that hasn't developed into a more personal interest?'

'Where on earth did you get the idea that Sam was interested in me in that way?' Erin demanded baldly.

'It's the way he looks at you sometimes, the way he takes advantage of any excuse to go and speak to you. The last time you were on leave he didn't know what to do with himself.'

Erin usually respected the worldly-wise Janice's opinions but on this particular issue she was convinced that the older woman had got it badly wrong. Erin was confident that she knew her boss inside out and would have noticed anything amiss. She was also mortified on Sam's behalf, for he was a very proper man with old-fashioned values, who would loathe the existence of such rumours on the staff grapevine. He had never flirted with Erin. Indeed he had never betrayed the smallest sign that he looked on Erin as anything other than a trusted and valued employee.

'I think you're wrong but I do hope that nobody else has the same suspicions about us.'

'That car will cause talk,' Janice warned her wryly. 'There's plenty people around here who will be happy to say that there's no fool like an old fool!'

Erin's face flamed. She was suddenly eager to bring the excruciating discussion to an end. She had grown extremely fond of Sam Morton and respected him as a self-made man with principles. Even talking about Sam as a man with the usual male appetites embarrassed her. Not only had the older man given her a chance to work for him when most people wouldn't have bothered, but he had also promoted and encouraged her ever since then. It was purely thanks to Sam that she had a decent career, a salary she could live on and good prospects. Only how good would those prospects be if Sam sold up and she got a new employer? A new owner would likely want to bring in his own staff and, even if he had to wait for the opportunity, she would not have the freedom to operate as she currently did. It was a sobering thought. Erin had heavy responsibilities on the home front and the mere thought of unemployment made her skin turn clammy and her tummy turn over sickeningly with dread.

'I'd better get on. Owen's interviewing therapists this afternoon,' Erin said ruefully. 'I don't want to keep him waiting.'

As Erin drove the sleek BMW several miles to reach the Black's Inn, the smallest property in Sam's portfolio—an elegant Georgian hotel, which incorporated a brand-new custom-built spa—she was thinking anxiously about how much money she had contrived to put by in savings in recent months. Not as much as she had hoped, certainly not nearly enough to cover her expenses in the event of job loss, she reflected worriedly. Unfortunately she could never forget the huge struggle she had had trying to get by on welfare benefits when her twins, Lorcan and Nuala, were newly born. Back then her mother, once so proud of her daughter's achievements, had been aghast at the mess Erin had made of her seemingly promising future. Erin had felt like a total failure and had worked out the exact moment that it had all gone belly up for her. It would have been great to have a terrific career *and* the guy of her dreams but possibly hoping for that winning combination had been downright greedy. In actuality she had fallen madly in love with the wrong guy and had taken her life apart to make it dovetail with his. All the lessons she had learned growing up had been forgotten, her ambitions put on hold, while she chased her dream lover.

And ever since then, Erin had been beating herself up for her mistakes. When she couldn't afford to buy something for the twins, when she had to listen in tolerant silence to her mother's regrets for the youthful freedom she had thrown away by becoming a single parent, she was painfully aware that she could only blame herself. She had precious little excuse for her foolishness and lack of foresight. After all, Erin had grown up in a poor home listening to her father talk endlessly and impressively about how he was going to make his fortune. Over and over and over again she had listened and the fortune had never come. Worse still, on many occasions money that could not be spared had been frittered away on crazy schemes and had dragged her family down into debt. By the time she was ten years old and watching her poorly educated mother work in a succession of dead-end jobs to keep her family solvent, she had realised that her father was just a dreamer, full of money-making ideas but lacking the work ethic required to bring any of those ideas to fruition. His vain belief that he was set on earth to shine as brightly as a star had precluded him from seeking an ordinary job. In any case working to increase someone else's profit had been what her idle father called 'a mug's game'. He had died in a train crash when she was twelve and from that point on life in her home had become less of a roller-coaster ride.

In short, Erin had learned at a young age that she needed to learn how best to keep herself and that it would be very risky to look to any man to take care of her. As a result, she had studied hard at school, ignored those who called her a nerd and gone on to university, also ignoring her mother's protestations that she should have moved straight into a job to earn a wage. Boyfriends had come and gone, mostly unremarked, for Erin had been wary of getting too involved, of compromising her ambitions to match someone else's. Having set her sights on a career with prospects, she had emerged from university with a top-flight business management degree. To help to finance her years as a student she had also worked every spare hour as a personal trainer, a vocation that had gained her a raft of more practical skills, not least on how best to please in a service industry.

Later that afternoon, when she returned from her visit to Black's Inn, the Stanwick receptionist informed Erin that Sam wanted to see her immediately. Realising in dismay that she had forgotten to switch her mobile phone back on after the interviews were finished, Erin knocked lightly on the door of her boss's office and walked straight in with the lack of ceremony that Sam preferred.

'Ah, Erin, at last. Where have you been all afternoon? There's someone here I want you to meet,' Sam informed her with just a hint of impatience.

'Sorry, I forgot to remind you that I'd be over at Black's doing interviews with Owen,' Erin explained, smiling apologetically until a movement by the window removed her attention from the older man. She turned her head and began to move forward, visually tracking the emergence of a tall powerful male from the shadows. Then she froze as though a glass wall had suddenly sprung into being around her, imprisoning her and shutting her off from her companions.

'Miss Turner?' a sleek cultured drawl with the suggestion of an accent purred. 'I've been looking forward to meeting you. Your boss speaks very highly of you.'

Erin flinched as though a thunderclap had sounded within the room without warning, that dark-timbred voice unleashing an instant 'fight or flight instinct she had to struggle to keep under control. She would have known that distinctive intonation laced with command had she heard it even at a crowded party. It was as unforgettable as the male himself.

'This is—' Sam began.

'Cristophe Donakis…' Cristo extended a lean brown hand to greet her as if they had never met before.

And Erin just stared in consternation at that wicked fallen-angel face as if she couldn't believe her eyes. And she *couldn't*. Cropped black hair spiky with the short curls that not even the closest cut could eradicate entirely, ebony brows level above stunning dark deep-set eyes that could turn as golden as the sunset, high cheekbones and, as though all the rest was not enough to over-endow him with beauty, a mouth that was the all-male sensual equivalent of pure temptation. The passage of time since their final encounter had left no physical mark on those lean dark features. In a split second it was as if she had turned her head and stepped back in time. He remained defiantly drop-dead gorgeous. Something low down in her body that she hadn't felt in years clenched tightly and uncomfortably, making her press her slender thighs together in dismay.

'Mr Donakis,' Erin pronounced woodenly, lifting her chin and very briefly touching his hand, determined to betray no reaction that Sam might question. Sam's 'big appointment' was with Cristo? She was horrified, fighting to conceal her reactions, could feel a soul-deep trembling begin somewhere in the region of her wobbly knees. That fast she was being bombarded by unwelcome images from their mutual past. Cristo grinning with triumph and punching the air when he finally beat her in a swimming race; Cristo serving her breakfast in bed when she was unwell and making a production of feeding her grapes one by one, long brown fingers caressing her lips at every opportunity, teaching her that no part of her was impervious to his touch. Cristo, sex personified night or day with an unashamedly one-track mind. He had taught her so much, *hurt* her so much she could hardly bear to look at him.

'Make it Cristo. I'm not a big fan of formality,' Cristo murmured levelly and even the air around him seemed cool as frost.

Just as suddenly Erin was angry, craving the power to knock him into the middle of next week for not being surprised by her appearance. Evidently he had known in advance that she worked for Sam and he was not prepared to own up to their previous relationship, which suited Erin perfectly. Indeed she was grateful that he had pretended she was a stranger, for she cringed at the idea of Sam and her colleagues learning what an idiot she had once been. One of Cristo Donakis' ex-girlfriends, *what*? That guy who changed women as he changed socks? *Really*? Inside her head she could already imagine the jeers and scornful amusement that that revelation would unleash, for Erin already knew that she had the reputation of being standoffish with the staff for keeping her private life private while others happily told all. Was Cristo the prospective buyer of Sam's hotels? For what other reason would he be visiting the Stanwick hotel? Cristo owned an international hotel and leisure empire.

'Erin…I'd like you to give Cristo a tour of our facilities here and at the other spas. His particular interest lies with them,' Sam told her equably. 'You can give him the most recent breakdown of figures. Believe me when I tell you that this girl has a mind like a computer for the important details.'

Erin went pink in receipt of that compliment.

'Looks *and* brains—I'm impressed,' Cristo pronounced with a slow smile that somehow contrived to freeze her to the marrow.

'You own the Donakis group,' Erin remarked tightly, trying to combat the shocked blankness of her mind with a shrewd take on what Cristo's source of interest could be in a trio of comparatively small hotels, which while luxurious could not seriously compare to the opulence of the elite Donakis hotel standards. 'I thought you specialised in city hotels.'

'My client base also enjoy country breaks. In any business there's always room for expansion in a new direction. I want to provide my clients with a choice of custom-made outlets so that they no longer have to patronise my competitors,' Cristo drawled smoothly.

'The beauty market is up-and-coming. What was once a treat for special occasions is now seen as a necessity by many women and by men as well,' Erin commented, earning an appreciative glance from her boss.

'You surprise me. I've never used a spa in my life,' Cristo proclaimed without hesitation.

'But your nails are filed and your brows are phenomenally well groomed,' Erin commented softly, earning a startled appraisal from Sam, who clearly feared that she was getting much too personal about his guest's grooming habits.

'You're very observant,' Cristo remarked silkily.

'Well, I have to be. One third of our customer base is male,' Erin fielded smoothly.

CHAPTER TWO

Erin escorted Cristo to the fitness suite that connected with the spa.

'You *can't* buy Sam's hotels,' she said tightly in an undertone, the words framed by gritted teeth. 'I don't want to work for you again.'

'Believe me, I don't want you on my payroll either,' Cristo declared with succinct bite.

Well, she knew how she could take that. If he took over, she would be out in the cold as soon as the law allowed such a move and, appalling as the prospect of unemployment was, it was a welcome warning at a moment when she was feeling far too hot and bothered to think straight. What was it about Cristophe Donakis? That insidious power of his that got to her every time? Sheathed in a charcoal grey pinstripe suit, fitted to his lean powerful body with the flare that only perfect tailoring could offer, Cristo looked spectacular and, although she very much wanted to be, she was not indifferent to his high-voltage sexual charge. Cristo was a very beautiful man with the sleek dark good looks of a Greek god. As she turned to look at him, eyes as blank as she could make them, there was a lowdown buzz already feeding through her every limb like poison. She knew what that buzz was and feared it deeply. It was the burn of excitement, gut-deep, breathtaking *excitement*.

'I wasn't expecting to find a gym here,' Cristo remarked, eying the banks of machines and their sweating occupants, swivelling his handsome head to glance through the glass partition to where a couple of men were training with heavy weights. He returned his attention to her just as Erin slicked her tongue across her white teeth as if she was seeking to eradicate a stray smudge of lipstick. She wasn't wearing very much, just a hint of pale pearlised gloss that added unnecessary voluptuousness to the full swell of that sultry mouth, which he was working very hard not to imagine moving against his... Don't go there, his cool intelligence cautioned him, acting to suppress the kind of promptings that would interfere with his concentration.

'An exercise suite dovetails perfectly with the spa. The customers come here to train and attend classes, treat themselves to a massage or a beauty treatment and go home feeling spoiled and refreshed.' As Erin talked she led the way into the spa and gave him a brief look at those facilities that were free for his appraisal. 'People have less free time these days. It makes sense to offer a complete package at the right price. The profits speak for themselves.'

'So, how much are you creaming off in reward for your great moneymaking ideas?' Cristo enquired smoothly.

Her brow furrowed, amethyst eyes flickering in confusion across his strong bronzed face. 'I don't get commission for bringing in more business,' she responded uncertainly.

'That wasn't what I meant and you know it. I've seen

enough of the premises here. We'll move on to Blacks now and fit in the last place before dinner,' he told her arrogantly.

Cristo strode out to the front of the hotel and the silver Bugatti Veyron sports car that was his pride and joy. Erin followed more slowly, her agile brain struggling to work out what he had meant. 'I'll take my own car,' she called in his wake, crossing to the BMW. 'Then I can go home without needing a lift.'

Cristo wheeled back in his tracks, brilliant dark eyes gleaming between lush curling lashes. He was quick to note the premium model that she drove and he wondered with derision just how she afforded such a vehicle. 'No, I'll take you. We have business to discuss.'

Erin could think of nothing she wanted to discuss with him and she wanted him nowhere near the home she shared with her mother but, as Sam's right-hand woman, keeping Cristo happy was paramount. She wanted Cristo to vanish in a puff of black smoke like the fallen angel he resembled but she did not want Sam to lose out because she hadn't done her job right: she owed the older man too much for his faith in her and could not have looked him in the eye again if she scared off Cristo to suit her own personal preferences. Yet was she capable of scaring him off? There was an air of purpose about Cristo that said otherwise. To be fair, Sam's busy hotels would make a good investment. She pulled out her phone to ring Owen, the manager at Black's, to give him notice of their intended visit.

With pronounced reluctance she climbed into Cristo's boy-toy car, trying not to recall the time she had attended the Motor Show with him where the beautiful models draped over the latest luxury cars had salivated every time Cristo came within touching distance. Women always *always* noticed Cristo, ensnared by his six-foot-four-inch height and breadth and the intensity of dark eyes that could glitter like black diamonds.

Out of the corner of his gaze, Cristo watched her clasp her hands on her lap and instantly he knew she was on edge, composing herself into the little concentrated pool of calm and silence she invariably embraced when she was upset. She was so damn small, a perfect little package at five feet two inches calculated to appeal to the average testosterone-driven male as a vulnerable female in need of masculine protection. His shapely mouth took on a sardonic slant as he accelerated down the drive. She could look after herself. He had once enjoyed her independent streak, the fact she didn't always come when he called. Like most men he preferred a challenge to a clinging vine but he knew how tricky she could be and had no intention of forgetting it.

Erin wanted to keep her tongue pinned to the roof of her mouth but she couldn't. 'What you said back there—that phrase you used, "creaming off," —I didn't like the connotations—'

'I didn't think you would,' Cristo fielded softly, his dark accented drawl vibrating low in his throat.

Gooseflesh covered the backs of her hands and suddenly she felt chilled. 'Were you getting at something?'

'What do you think?'

'Don't play games with me,' she urged, breathing in deep and slow, nostrils flaring in dismay at the familiar spicy scent of his designer aftershave.

The smell of him, so familiar, so *achingly* familiar, unleashed a tide of memories. When he was away from her she used to sleep in one of his shirts but she would never have done anything so naff and revealing when he was around. Sometimes when she was at his city apartment she used to wash his shirts as well, she recalled numbly, eager to take on any little homely task that could made her feel more like one half of a committed couple. But Cristo had *not* made a commitment to her, had not done anything to make her feel secure and had never once mentioned love or the future. Recalling those hard facts, she wondered why she had once looked back on that phase as being the happiest of her life. Admittedly that year with Cristo had been the most exciting, varied and challenging of her twenty-five years of existence but the moments of happiness had often been fleeting and she had passed a great deal more time worrying about where their affair was going and never daring to ask. She had worked so hard at playing it cool with him, on not attaching strings or expectations that might irritate him. Her soft full mouth turned down at the recollection—much good all that anxious stressing and striving had done her! At the end of the day, in spite of all her precautions, he had still walked away untouched while she had been crushed in the process. She had had to accept that all along she had only been a Miss All-Right-For-Now on his terms, not a woman he was likely to stay with. No, she was just one more in a long line of women who had contrived to catch his eye and entertain him for a while until the time came for him to choose a suitable wife. The knowledge that she had meant so little to him that he had ditched her to marry another woman still burned like acid inside her.

'Maybe I'm hoping you'll finally come clean,' Cristo murmured levelly.

Erin turned her head, smooth brow indented with a

frown as she struggled to recall the conversation and get back into it again. 'Come clean about what?'

Cristo pulled off the road into a layby before he responded. 'I found out what you were up to while you were working for me at the Mobila spa.'

Erin twisted her entire body round to look at him, crystalline eyes flaring bright, her rising tension etched in the taut set of her heart-shaped face. 'What do you mean, what I was up to?'

Cristo flexed long brown fingers round the steering wheel and then turned to look at her levelly, ebony dark eyes cool and opaque as frosted glass. 'You were helping yourself to the profits in a variety of inventive ways but I employ a forensic accounting team, who have seen it all before, and they traced the transactions back to you. You were *stealing* from me.'

For a split second, Erin was pinned to the seat by the sheer weight of her incredulity and her eyes were huge. 'That's an outrageous and disgusting lie!' she slammed back at him, her voice rising half an octave with a volume stirred by simple shock.

'I have the proof and witnesses,' Cristo breathed in a tone of cutting finality that brooked no argument, igniting the engine again and filtering the car back onto the main road without batting an eyelash.

'You can't have proof and witnesses for something that never happened!' Erin launched at him furiously. 'I can't believe that you can accuse me of something like that—I've never stolen anything in my life!'

'You *stole* from me,' Cristo shot back at her with simmering emphasis, his bold bronzed profile hard as iron. 'You can't argue with hard evidence.'

Erin was stunned, not only by the accusation coming

so long after the event and out of nowhere at her, but by the rock-solid assurance of his conviction in her guilt.

'I don't care what evidence you think you've got. As it never happened, as I never helped myself to anything I wasn't entitled to, the evidence can only have been manufactured!'

'Nothing was manufactured. Face facts. You got greedy and you got caught,' Cristo asserted grittily. 'I'd have had you charged with theft if I'd known where to find you but by the time I found out you were long gone.'

Trembling with frustrated fury, every nerve jangling with adrenalin, Erin waited impatiently for him to park outside the nineteen-thirties black and white frontage of the Black's Inn hotel. Then she wrenched at the handle on the passenger door and leapt out. Cristo watched her through the windscreen, bleakly amused by the angry heat in her shaken face. She was shocked that he had found her out and not surprisingly frantic to convince him that she was as innocent as a newborn lamb of the charges. Naturally she wouldn't want him to label her a thief with her current employer. Even if she *had* resisted temptation this time around, mud stuck and no boss could have a faith in a member of staff with such a fatal weakness.

Slowly and with the easy moving fluidity of a natural athlete, Cristo climbed out of the car and locked it.

Erin's small hands clenched into fists at her side as she squared up to him. 'We're going to have this out!'

Infuriatingly in control, Cristo cast her a slumberous glance from below his ridiculously long lashes. 'Not a good idea in a public place—'

'We'll borrow Owen's office.' Erin stalked into the hotel and saw the lanky blond manager already on his way out to welcome them. She hurried over to him. 'We'll do the tour in ten minutes. Right now we need somewhere private to talk. Could we use your office?'

'Of course.' Owen spread the door wide and as she passed him smiled down at her and whispered, 'By the way, thanks for the heads-up.'

Cristo noticed that friendly little exchange but not its content and wondered at the precise nature of Erin's relationship with the handsome young manager. Generally she liked older men, Cristo reflected until he recalled the youth barely, if even, into his twenties that he had surprised in her hotel bed and his expressive mouth clenched hard. He recalled Sam Morton's gushing praise of his beautiful area manager and his derision rose even higher. He doubted that he'd ever met a man more in a woman's thrall. Sam thought the sun, the moon and the stars rose on Erin Turner.

Erin closed the door on Cristo's entry and spun back to him, amethyst eyes dark with anger. 'I am not a thief, so naturally I want to know exactly why you're making these allegations.'

He studied her with narrowed eyes. She was breathing fast, her silky top sliding tantalisingly against the rounded bulge of her breasts. Creamy lickable mounds topped by succulent strawberry nipples, he remembered lasciviously, his desire firing at that imagery as a bolt of lust shot through him in a flash, leaving him hard as a rock. What she lacked in height she more than made up for with wonderfully feminine curves. He had loved her body. Even worse, he had dreamt of her passion when he was away from her, craving the unparalleled sexual satisfaction he had yet to find with anyone else.

'I'm not an idiot,' Cristo informed her coldly, forcing

his keen mind back to a safer pathway. 'At the Mobila spa, you sold products out of the beauty store on your own behalf, falsified invoices and paid therapists who didn't exist. Your fraudulent acts netted you something in the region of twenty grand in a comparatively short time frame. How could you think that that level of deceit would go unnoticed?'

'I am not a thief,' Erin repeated doggedly although an alarm bell had gone off in her head the instant he mentioned the theft and sale of products from the store.

She knew someone who had done that for she herself had actually caught the woman putting a box of products into her car. Sally, her administrative assistant in the office, whom she had relied on heavily at the time, had been stealing and selling the exclusive items online. Unfortunately Erin had no proof of that fact because she had neither called in the police to handle the matter nor shared the truth that Sally had been stealing with another member of staff. Instead she had sat a distraught Sally down to talk to her. Together the two women had then done a stocktake and Erin had ended up replacing the missing products out of her own pocket. Why? She had felt desperately sorry for the older woman, struggling to cope alone with two autistic children after her husband had walked out on her. But had she only scraped the tip of the iceberg when it came to Sally's dishonesty? Had Sally even then been engaged in rather more imaginative methods of gaining money by duplicitous means?

'I have the proof,' Cristo retorted crisply.

'And witnesses, you said,' Erin recalled. 'Would one of those witnesses be Sally Jennings?'

His lean strong face tightened and she knew she had

hit a nerve. 'You can't talk or charm your way out of this, Erin—'

'I'm not interested in charming you. I'm not the same woman I was when we were together,' Erin countered curtly, for what he had done to her had toughened her. There was nothing like surviving an unhappy love affair to build self-knowledge and character, she reckoned painfully. He had broken her heart, taught her how fragile she was, left her bitter and humiliated. But she had had to pick herself up again fast once she discovered that she was pregnant. Choice and self-pity hadn't come into that challenging equation.

Erin stared back at him, pale amethyst eyes searching his darkly handsome features, blocking her instinctive response to that beautiful bone structure. Had he truly not read a single one of her letters? What had happened to human curiosity? Her phone calls had gone unanswered and his PA had told her she was wasting her time phoning because Cristo wouldn't accept a call from her. Even when she had got desperate enough to call his family home in Greece she had run into a brick wall erected by his spiteful foster mother, who had proudly told her that Cristo was getting married and wanted nothing more to do with, 'a woman like her'. As if she were some trollop Cristo had picked up in the street for a night of sex, rather than the woman who had been his constant companion for a year.

Although, perhaps it hadn't been his foster mother's fault. After all, while she might have seen herself in the light of a serious relationship, it was clear that Cristo had seen her entirely differently. He had never let her meet his family and, even though he'd known that she wanted him to meet her mother, he had found it inconvenient every time she'd tried to set up even a casual encounter. She might have been part of his private life but he had walled her off from everyone else in it, for she had only occasionally met his friends and never again after the evening when one of his mates had made a point of commenting on how long he had been with Erin.

'I think you'll change your tune once you appreciate how few choices you have,' Cristo responded softly. 'Now let's view the facilities here. I have a tight schedule.'

Her mouth tightening, she followed him out of the office. How did he expect her to change her tune? Certainly, he hadn't listened to a word she'd said. Had Sally Jennings lied about her? What else could she think? Had her abrupt departure from her job at the Mobila spa played right into the older woman's hands when the irregularities were exposed by the accounting team? Change her tune? What had he meant by that comment? Her brain engaged in working out what she could possibly do to combat such allegations, Erin realised that she would have to see the evidence he had mentioned to work out her own defence and how to nail the real culprit. Had she been a total idiot to let Sally off the hook when she caught her stealing? She was appalled that her sympathetic and supportive treatment of the older woman might have been repaid with lies calculated to make Erin look guilty in her place. Confronting Sally, appealing to her conscience—if she had one—might well be the only course she could take. But what had Cristo meant about choices?

Owen brimmed with enthusiasm as he showed them round the spa, describing the latest improvements and special offers as well as the upsurge in custom that had resulted. He finished by offering them coffee but Cristo demurred, pleading time constraints as he whisked Erin back out to the car and angled it back out onto the road to make their last call. Brackens was Sam's most exclusive property. A Victorian house set in wooded surroundings, it was very popular with couples in search of a romantic weekend and the spa was run as a member's only club.

Erin watched Mia, the elegant brunette in her thirties who managed Brackens, melt at Cristo's first smile and allowed the knowledgeable manager to do most of the talking as she showed them round her impressive domain. Erin was struggling to concentrate on the job at hand. There was too much else on her bemused mind. So, for almost three years, Cristo had been under the impression that she had stolen a fat wad of cash from him. Why hadn't he contacted her? Why had he virtually let it go instead of informing the police? Cristo never let people get away with doing the dirty on him. He was a man few would wish to cross but he did reward loyal, hardworking staff with generous bonuses and opportunities.

Watching Mia laugh flirtatiously with Cristo made Erin feel slightly nauseous. She could recall when she had been even more impressionable. One glance at that lean dark face of sharp angles and creative hollows and those stunning black diamond eyes and she had been enamoured, her interest caught, her body humming with unfamiliar thrills. Her wariness with men, her long hours of study while others partied, had made her more than usually vulnerable for a young woman of twenty-one. She slammed down hard on the memory, awarding Cristo a veiled glance when he ushered her back to his Bugatti with a fleeting remark on her quietness.

'May I go home now?' she enquired as he turned the sports car.

'We're having dinner together at my hotel,' Cristo informed her. 'We have things to talk about.'

'I have nothing to talk to you about. Sam does his own negotiating,' Erin volunteered drily. 'I'm just the hired help.'

'If rumour is to be believed, you're not *just* anything when it comes to Sam Morton.'

Erin went rigid in the passenger seat at the suggestion. 'Do you listen to rumours?'

'You slept with me while I was employing you,' Cristo reminded her without heat.

Her teeth ground together. For two pins she would have slapped him. 'That's different. We were already involved when I began working for you.'

Cristo compressed his beautifully shaped mouth, his thoughts taking him back even though he didn't want to go there. He had never had to work so hard to get a woman into bed. Her elusiveness, her surprising inhibitions had heightened his desire, persuaded him that she was different. Yes, she *had* been different, she had lined her pockets at his expense throughout their affair, he recalled grimly. She had taken him for a fool just as she was taking Morton.

'Sam and I are only friends—'

His eloquent mouth quirked. 'The same sort of friendship you had with that other friend of yours, Tom?'

Erin stiffened, remembering how suspicious Cristo had become of her fondness for Tom's company towards the end of their affair. 'Not as familiar. Sam's from a different generation.'

Tom was a mate from her university days, more like a brother than anything else and still an appreciated part of Erin's life. Unfortunately Cristo didn't believe that platonic friendships could exist and Erin had eventually given up trying to convince him otherwise, reasoning that she was entitled to her own friends regardless of his opinions.

'Morton's old enough to be your grandfather—'

'Which is why there's nothing else between us,' Erin slotted in flatly. 'I'm not sleeping with Sam.'

'He's besotted with you. I don't believe you,' Cristo framed succinctly.

'That's your prerogative.' Erin dug out her mobile phone and tapped out her home number.

Her mother answered. In the background she could hear a child crying. Lorcan, she guessed. Her son sounded tired and cross and her heart clenched, for she felt guilty that she couldn't be there with him. It hurt that she got to spend so little time with her children during the week and she cherished her weekends with the twins when she tried to make up for her absence during working hours.

'I'm sorry but I'll be late home tonight,' she told Deidre Turner.

'Why? What are you doing?' the older woman asked.

'I have some work to deal with before I can leave.'

Tight-lipped and knowing she still had a maternal interrogation to face, Erin put her phone back in her bag. The very last thing she could afford to tell her parent was that Cristo had reappeared in her life. She would never hear the end of it, much as she had yet to hear the end of the reproaches about bringing two children into the world without first having acquired a wedding ring on her finger. But she didn't blame her mother for her attitude. Educated in a convent school by nuns and deeply devout, Deidre had somewhat rigid views. At the same time, however, she was a very loving and caring grandmother and Erin could not have coped as a single parent without the older woman's support.

'I still don't know what this is about,' Erin complained as Cristo parked outside the foremost hotel in the area. 'I didn't steal from you three years ago but until you give me more facts I can't defend myself.'

'One of the transactions was traced right back to your bank account. Don't waste your time trying to plead innocence,' Cristo shot back at her very drily.

'I don't want to have dinner with you. It's not like we parted on good terms,' Erin reminded him doggedly.

Cristo climbed gracefully out of the car. 'It's like this. Either you dine with me and we talk or I go straight to your boss with my file on your thefts.'

He spoke so levelly, so unemotionally that for several taut seconds Erin could not quite accept that he had threatened her without turning a hair. The blood drained from below her fair skin and she froze until she recognised that he had given her a choice. She could tell him to take his precious file of supposed evidence and put it where the sun didn't shine. She could call his bluff. But, unhappily for her, she *knew* Cristophe Donakis and she knew what he was capable of.

He didn't bluff and he was very determined. He would push to the limits and beyond to gain a desired result. He was tough, sufficiently volatile to be downright dangerous and a merciless enemy. If Cristo truly

CHAPTER THREE

ERIN walked into the cloakroom of the hotel and ran her wrists below the cold water tap until the panicked thump of her heartbeat seemed to slow to a tolerable level. Get a grip on yourself, she told her tense reflection as she dried her hands. Why should Cristo come back into her life now and try to wreck it? On his part it would be a pointless exercise…

Unless he *was* after revenge. At the vanity counter she tidied her hair and noticed with annoyance that her hands were no longer steady. He had already contrived to wind her up like a clockwork toy, firing all her self-defence mechanisms into override. And she needed to watch out because panic would make her stupid and careless. She breathed in slow and deep, fighting to stay calm. He didn't know about the children so evidently he had not read a single one of her letters. Had he known about the twins he would have left her in peace, she was convinced of it. What man went out of his way to dig up trouble?

Cristo did, a little voice piped up warningly at the back of her head, and all of a sudden time was taking her back to their first encounter.

At the time Erin was employed in her first job as a

deputy manager at a council leisure centre. Elaine, one of her university friends, was from a wealthy home and her father had bought her an apartment in an exclusive building. When Elaine realised what a struggle Erin was having trying to find decent accommodation on a budget, she had offered Erin her box room, a space barely large enough for a single bed with storage beneath. But Erin hadn't cared how small the room was, she had enjoyed having Elaine's company, not to mention daily access to the residents' fancy leisure complex on the ground floor.

Erin had always been a keen swimmer and had won so many trophies for her school that she could have aspired to an athletic career had her parents been of a different ilk. Regretfully, in spite of her coach's efforts at persuasion, Erin's parents had been unwilling to commit to the time and cost of supporting a serious training schedule for their talented daughter. However, Erin still loved the sport and swam as often as she could.

The first time she had seen Cristo he had been scything up and down the pool with the sleek flow of a shark. His technique had been lazy, his speed moderate, she had noted, overtaking him without effort as she pursued her usual vigorous workout.

'Race me!' he had challenged when he caught up with her.

And she still recalled those dark deep-set gorgeous eyes, gleaming like polished bronze, electrifying in his lean, darkly handsome features.

'I'll beat you,' she warned him ruefully. 'Can you take that?'

The dark golden eyes had flashed as though she had lit a fire inside him. 'Bring it on…' he had urged.

And just like him, she had loved the challenge, skimming through the water with the firing power of a bullet, beating him to the finish line and turning to cherish his look of disbelief. Afterwards she had hauled herself out of the water and he had followed suit, straightening his lean powerful length to tower over her diminutive frame, water streaming down over his six-pack abs, drawing her attention to his superb muscular development. It was possibly the very first time that she had ever *seriously* noticed a man's body.

'You're tiny. How the hell did you beat me?' he demanded incredulously.

'I'm a good swimmer.'

'We have to have a retrial, *koukla mou.*'

'OK, same time Wednesday night but I warn you I train every day and your technique is sloppy—'

'Sloppy…' Cristo repeated in accented disbelief, an ebony brow quirking. 'If I wasn't tired, I'd have beaten you hollow!'

Erin laughed. 'Sure you would,' she agreed peaceably, knowing what the male ego was like.

He extended a lean brown hand. 'I'm Cristophe Donakis…I'll see you Wednesday and I'll whip your hide.'

'I don't think so,' she told him cheerfully.

'Cristophe Donakis? You met Cristophe in the residents' pool where us ordinary people swim?' Elaine later gasped in consternation. 'What on earth was he doing there? He owns the penthouse and he has a private pool on the roof.'

'Well, he was slumming this evening. Who is he?'

'A spoilt rotten Greek tycoon and playboy with pots of money and a different woman on the go every week. I've seen him taking them up there in the lift. He's very fond of decorative beauties. Stay clear. He'd gobble you up like a mid-morning snack,' Elaine warned her drily.

But that same night the recollection of Cristo's flawless male perfection got Erin all hot and bothered in her dreams and she marvelled that he could have that effect on her, for her strict upbringing had made her reserved and wary about all things sexual. Even at a glance she had recognised that Cristophe Donakis was a very sexual animal. On the Wednesday she beat him a second time, albeit with a little more effort on her part.

'Join me for a drink,' he suggested afterwards, his hungry gaze wandering at leisure over her slim curves in the plain black and red suit she wore, rising to linger on her soft full mouth, the sexual charge of his interest blatant and bringing self-conscious colour to her cheeks.

'No, thanks.' Fear of getting out of her depth and of somehow making a fool of herself made Erin especially cautious

'A rematch, then…third time lucky?' he prompted, amusement dancing in his stunning eyes below the fringe of black curling lashes.

'My flatmate tells me you have your own pool.'

'It's in the process of being replaced. Rematch?' he pressed again, pure challenge gleaming in those bronzed eyes. 'The next time the loser buys dinner. Give me your phone number and we'll arrange a date for it. I'm about to leave for the US for a week.'

She admired his persistence and had never been able to resist a dare. The third time he beat her, punching the air with uninhibited triumph. And that was also the moment she fell for Cristo, loving the naturally dramatic streak that he kept concealed below the surface in favour of cool assurance and the gloriously wicked grin that could burnish his hard dark features with adorably boyish enthusiasm.

She fed him in an American-style diner down the street in the sort of basic unsophisticated setting that she could tell was unfamiliar to him, but he proved a good sport and an entertaining raconteur, who drew her out about her job and her ambitions. He assumed that she would accompany him back to his apartment after the meal, looked at her in frank surprise when she refused, for he was very much a male accustomed to easy conquests. After that rebuff it took him two whole weeks to phone her again.

'He'll hurt you,' Elaine forecast. 'He's too handsome, too rich, too arrogant. You're very down to earth. What have you got in common with a guy like that?'

And the answer was…*nothing*. But like a moth drawn to a candle flame she had refused to acknowledge the obvious and eventually she had got burned, badly enough burned to avoid getting involved ever since. From time to time other men had made a play for her but she had resisted, reluctant to entertain such a complication in her life. In any case living under the same roof as her mother was almost as good as wearing a chastity belt, she reflected with sheepish amusement.

Cristo was already seated in the elegant restaurant. He levered upright as she approached, his keen dark gaze welded to her delicate features. She looked like an angel, fragile, pure, amethyst eyes luminous as jewels in her heart-shaped face. He noticed the other men following her progress and the seductive image of her spread across his silk sheets flashed through his head, instantly hardening him. He marvelled at the effect she had on him even though he knew that she was both dishonest and untrustworthy, a thoughtless, foolish little slut below the patina of that perfection. No truly clever woman would have tossed him and what he could buy her away for the cheap thrill of a casual encounter and what he considered to be a paltry sum of money.

Erin felt the heat of his appraisal and flushed, her spine stiffening, her bone structure tightening as she exerted fierce self-discipline. Willing herself not to react, she sat down and immediately lifted the menu to peruse it. She picked a single course, told him that she didn't want any wine and sat as straight as a child told to sit properly at table.

'So, tell me what you want and get it over with,' she suggested, eager to take charge of the conversation rather than sit there quailing like a victim.

His dark golden eyes rested on the hands she had clasped together on the table top and his beautiful mouth took on a sardonic twist. 'I want you,' he countered levelly.

Her smooth brow indented. 'In what way?'

Cristo laughed, raw amusement lightening his stunning eyes to a shade somewhere between amber and honey. 'In the most obvious way that a man wants a woman.'

But she couldn't credit that, for hadn't he ditched her and moved on to marry an exceptionally beautiful Greek woman, a socialite called Lisandra, within weeks of their split? She hadn't been able to hold him then, hadn't been important enough to him to retain his interest. He had moved on with his life without her at breathtaking speed. Now he was divorced and it was mean of her to reflect that his marriage had barely lasted long enough for the ink to dry on the licence. Maybe he had got bored with his wife and being married in the same way that he had got bored with Erin. Maybe he didn't have what it took to really *care* about any woman.

'That's the price of my silence,' Cristo drawled smooth as silk.

Blackmail? Erin was shocked, so shocked that her teeth settled into the soft underside of her lower lip and she tasted the faint coppery tang of blood in her mouth. 'The silence relating to this supposed thieving you believe me to be guilty of—'

'*Know* you to be guilty of,' Cristo traded.

'You can't possibly be serious,' Erin breathed tightly.

Lean bronzed face radiating raw assurance, Cristo ran a lean brown forefinger down over the back of her hand and every skin cell in her body leapt into tingling awareness. 'Why would you think that? We had a very good time between the sheets.'

Assailed by unwelcome memories, Erin went rigid but that fast, still shockingly attuned to a certain dark intimate note in his deep drawl, her body reacted. Inside her bra, her breasts swelled, her nipples tightening into prominent points, and her breath rasped in her tight throat. She blinked, lashes lowering, shutting out the hot dark golden gaze pinned to her. He could still get to her and that shocked her but was it so surprising? She had lived like a nun since her children were born, grateful just to have a job and a roof over her head in the wake of the struggle to survive while she was pregnant and unemployed. *A good time.* That phrase cheapened her, made light of what she had once believed they had shared. Was a good time all she had been? Or was the very fact that he was back in her life, trying to force her to give him her time and her body again, proof that she had actually meant something more to him? It was a heady suspicion. Not that she still cared about him, she reflected, but like any woman she had her pride.

'So what are you suggesting?' Erin queried, resolving to play him along for a while until she better understood her position. 'Are you asking me to come back to you?'

'*Na pas sto dialo*…go to hell!' Cristo growled, incredulity flashing across his spectacular bone structure at that explosive suggestion. 'I'm talking about one weekend.'

Her delicate face froze tight. She felt the painful sting of that contempt right down to her marrow bone and inwardly swore that somehow, some way, some day he would pay for insulting her like that. Had the waiter not arrived with their meals she could not have trusted herself not to say something unwise. Forced to hold her tongue, she studied her plate fixedly, her hackles raised, bitterness poisoning her. How dared he? How dared he treat her like some hooker he could rent for an hour or two?

'A dirty weekend,' she framed through compressed lips. 'That does fit your MO.'

Those lustrous amber eyes shimmered below his thick sooty lashes, the leashed power of his strong personality and masculine virility creating an aggressive aura. Another punch of awareness slid through her. It was like poking a tiger through the bars of a cage and shockingly exciting, a welcome respite from the hard little knot of humiliation he had inflicted.

'One weekend in return for my silence and the twenty grand you stole…cheap at the price,' Cristo quipped cool as ice.

Erin wanted to thump him for that crack and restraining that natural urge made her slender hands clench into fists where she had placed them on her lap, out of view of his shrewd notice. The only way to play it with Cristo was cool. If she lost her temper she was lost and he would walk all over her.

'Stop playing the ice goddess. That may be a turn on for Morton but it doesn't rev my engine at all,' Cristo informed her drily. 'One weekend—that's the deal on the table—'

'Was this whole thing a set-up? Have you no intention of buying Sam out?' Erin pressed shakily.

'That is a question for me and my acquisitions team to decide. If it's a good investment your presence on the staff will not deter me, although obviously I'd be bringing back the forensic accounting team to run a check on your activities.'

Her chin came up. 'They'll find nothing because I have done nothing dishonest. Neither at Sam's company nor at yours. Furthermore I will not accept blackmail.'

'I think you'll end up eating those words,' Cristo forecast gently, spearing a chunk of succulent steak, primal male to the bone in his unspoilt appetite.

'You have to show me the evidence you say you have before I can make any kind of a decision.'

'After we've eaten. It's in my suite,' he responded equably.

His easy acquiescence on that score shook Erin. Clearly he was confident about the proof he had of her deceit. But, dismayed though she was by that suspicion, she brought her chin up, amethyst eyes glinting with challenge. 'We'll see.'

And she ate even though she wasn't hungry, for to push her food round her plate and leave it virtually untouched would only highlight the reality that she was sick with nerves.

'I have to go home for a week,' Cristo told her smoothly. 'My foster father's company is in trouble and he needs my advice. You must be aware of the state of the Greek economy.'

Erin nodded grudgingly. 'Aren't you suffering from the same effects?'

'My businesses are primarily here and in North America. I saw the way things were going a couple of years back but Vasos is stubborn. He dislikes change and he wouldn't listen to me when I tried to warn him.'

'And you are telling me this...*because*?'

'To help you to pen that weekend slot into your no doubt busy social calendar.'

Her teeth gritted behind her closed lips, her aggrieved sense of outrage building higher. He was so confident of winning that it was an affront. For a split second she was tempted to tell him that two young children took a heavy toll on what free time she had, but common sense kept her quiet, not to mention pride. She did not want him to know that a night out for her these days would most likely encompass a trip to the cinema or a modest meal with friends.

'So what is the state of play with Morton?' Cristo enquired quietly.

As Cristo was rarely quiet, she glanced up suspiciously. 'My relationship with Sam is none of your business.'

'I'm divorced,' he murmured flatly.

Erin shrugged a slim shoulder as if the information meant nothing to her. 'I read about it in the papers. Your marriage didn't last very long.'

He frowned, black brows drawing together. 'Long enough.'

And as his darkly handsome features shadowed and hardened Erin made a discovery that stung her. His broken marriage was still a source of discomfort to him. She sensed his regret and his reserve and the latter was nothing new. Cristo had always played his cards close to his chest, keeping his feelings under cover, and he had played it that way right to the end of their affair when he had told her it had run its course without drama or remorse. The recollection stiffened her backbone because she had been so shocked and unprepared for that development. This time around, she knew who and what she was dealing with: if he wanted a fight, one way or another, she would give him one!

They travelled up in the lift in a tense silence. She could not credit the situation she found herself in. Was she to be the equivalent of a rebound affair in the wake of his divorce? It occurred to her that a sleazy one-off weekend scarcely qualified for that lofty description and mortified pink highlighted her cheeks. Cristo studied her, picturing her silver gilt hair loose, a party dress to replace the business suit, high heels to show off those shapely legs. His body quickened to the image and was swiftly encouraged by far more X-rated images from the past. When he had her in his bed again, she would disappoint him, of course she would. It would not be as good as he remembered, he told himself urgently. That was the whole point of the game, that and, of course, a well-deserved dose of retribution. She had changed though. Those amethyst eyes no longer telegraphed every reaction making her easily read and she was more controlled than he recalled. Once she saw that he had definitive evidence of her thefts, she would surely study to please…

Erin had not quite bargained on the silent isolation of a hotel suite and she hovered in the centre of the reception room, having refused a drink. She watched him stride into the bedroom to retrieve whatever he was after, that long, lean, powerful body that had once haunted her dreams and ensured that other men could not compare so graceful in movement that she compressed her lips into a tight line, infuriated by the fact that she had noticed. But Cristo was a very noticeable guy. Every female head turned when he walked by and their attention lingered. But, Elaine had been right about him, he was a predator to the backbone and she was now simply a target with an X marked on her back. She wondered what his wife had done to him. Did Cristo have a score to settle against the female sex? And why, after almost three years had passed, was she on the menu again?

Cristo extended a file. 'Go ahead and take a look.'

Once again his self-assurance ignited her anxiety level. She took the file over to a sofa and sat down, determined not to be hurried or harassed. There were copies of many documents she had signed off while she worked for him, payments to suppliers and therapists, invoices attached to other copies that differed to show altered figures on the base lines. Her heart sank like lead in her chest and she felt as though someone were sitting on her lungs. It was very comprehensive stuff and shatteringly straightforward in its presentation.

Her knees developed an irritating tremor below the file on her lap but she still fought for a clear head. 'And

according to your investigation these particular therapists didn't exist?'

'You know they didn't,' Cristo responded flatly.

Erin came to the final document and stared down
at the evidence of a single large payment of a thou-
sand pounds heading into a bank account in her name
and nausea stirred in her stomach. Had she ever bothered to close that old bank account? She had intended
to but couldn't remember. Only one payment but one
was enough to damn her. In her opinion only Sally
Jennings could be responsible for such duplicity. She
had pretty much automatically signed anything that the
older woman put on her desk. With hindsight she knew
she had been too trusting. Unhappily managing the spa
had been her first serious job and she had had no deputy
to stand in for her when Cristo wanted her to make time
for him. Torn between too much work, hostile staff, who
loathed working for the owner's girlfriend, and a deep
driving desire to impress Cristo with her efficiency, she
had relied a lot on Sally, who had worked at the spa since
it had opened ten years earlier and knew the business
inside out. No such thing as a free ride, Erin told herself heavily now. Even Sam would doubt her innocence
in the face of such damning proof as the file contained.

Erin stood up and dropped the file down with a dis-
tasteful clunk of dismissal on the coffee table. 'Very
impressive, but I didn't *do* it! You gave me a great opportunity when you put me in that job and I wouldn't
have gone behind your back to steal from you.'

Cristo continued to stare at her, eyes like chips of
bright gold below his luxuriant lashes, and all of a sudden she was struggling to breathe evenly and something
inside her seemed to speed up as if her blood were rac-

ing through her veins and the buzz of forbidden excitement in the pit of her tummy were spreading like contagion to her entire body.

'You still want me, *koukla mou*,' Cristo purred, revelling in the charge in the atmosphere, the awareness in her clear gaze. It was the first time he had been able to read her again and it satisfied him.

'No! That is absolutely not true!' Erin shot back at him vehemently, wishing she had not asked to see that evidence in his presence as she recognised how much it had unnerved her and damaged her self-discipline. Now she was all shaken and stirred, a state to be avoided in a predator's radius.

Cristo reached out a hand and curled his fingers around her slender wrist, edging her out from behind the table. The storm of reaction inside her rose to hurricane force, suppressing her caution and defensiveness.

'No…' she said in a small choked voice, fighting just to get air back into her lungs.

Nevertheless he drew her close, banding strong arms round her like a prison, and the heat and strength of him acted like an aphrodisiac on her disturbed senses. She tried to keep distance between them, her slender body rigid as a rock, but he closed the gap with inexorable purpose.

'It's OK,' he rasped in the most frighteningly soothing tone. 'I want you too.'

And Erin did not want to hear that from the male who had dumped her and gone straight off to marry another woman. He had never wanted her enough to love her or keep her and that was the only wanting she had ever needed from him. He meant sex, only sex, she told herself feverishly while the reassuring warmth of him filtered through their clothing to warm her chilled limbs. But far more insidious was the insanely familiar smell of him that close, her nostrils flaring on the faint aroma of the same designer cologne he had always worn, never forgotten, and she was breathing him headily in as though he were a forbidden drug.

'Stop it, Cristo!' she told him tartly. 'I am not going there again. I am never going there again with you!'

'We'll see…' And, golden eyes blazing down at the fiercely conflicted expression on her heart-shaped face, his beautiful mouth swooped down on hers to claim the kiss she would have done almost anything to deny him.

And the taste of him was instantly addictive even as her hands swept up to strike in fists against his broad shoulders while he hauled her closer. Hot, hungry need roared through her in a storm that made her knees shake and she didn't know whether it was her or him behind it, or if, indeed, both of them were equally responsible. His tongue delved and she shuddered, so awake and defenceless against his every seductive move that it hurt, hurt to feel anything so strongly after so long without it. She wanted that kiss then with a sudden ferocity that terrified her. Nothing else mattered but the forceful power of that lean strong body against her own, the pulsing prominence of her nipples and the liquid burn between her thighs driving her on. His mouth bore down on hers with a seething, sizzling urgency that zinged through her slight length like an electric shock, stunning every sense into reaction. Nothing had ever tasted so good, nothing had ever felt so necessary and answering the shrill shriek of warning firing at the back of her brain took every atom of her inner strength.

'No!' she said in fierce rebuttal, thrusting him away

from her with an abruptness that almost made him lose that famous catlike balance of his as he backed into a chair.

In a daze, Cristo blinked. She packed a punch like a world-class boxer. He shook his handsome dark head, dark eyes instantly veiling as he fought the bite of unsated hunger clawing through his big powerful frame. 'You're right…this is not the moment. I have a flight to catch,' he retorted thickly.

Erin's breasts heaved as she frantically breathed in deep in an effort to emulate his fast recovery. Her amethyst eyes were dark with strong emotion as she studied his lean, darkly handsome features with a loathing she couldn't hide. 'I meant no as in *never*,' she contradicted shakily. 'Leave me alone, stay out of my life and stop threatening me.'

His black diamond eyes flared brilliant gold again, for there was nothing in life that Cristo enjoyed so much as a challenge. 'I won't go away.'

'You're going to get burned if you keep pushing me,' Erin warned him angrily, her small face set like a stone, all emotion but anger repressed. 'Get back out of my life or you'll regret it.'

'No, I won't. I rarely regret anything that I do,' Cristo fielded, visibly savouring the admission. 'Are you worried that I'll screw up your future with Morton? Sorry, *koukla mou*. I'll be doing him a favour. You're toxic.'

Her hands clenched into tight fists. 'I think you'll feel the toxic effect more strongly by the time this is over.'

Cristo shot her a grimly amused appraisal. 'I could handle you with one hand tied behind my back.'

'You always did like to believe your own publicity,' Erin countered tightly, her spine as straight as an arrow as she walked to the door. 'I'll catch a taxi back to Stanwick.'

In the lift, she had what felt like a panic attack, her heart beating too fast for comfort, cold clamminess filming her skin. That kiss? Total dynamite! How could that be? How had that happened? She was not in love with him any more, had believed she was fully cured of all that foolishness...until the instant she laid eyes on him again and his mesmerising attraction gripped her as tightly as steel handcuffs.

Maybe she'd succumbed to that kiss because she had been upset after reading that file. Is that the best excuse you can find? a little voice sneered inside her brain. She reddened, hating herself almost as much as she now hated him. Her response to him had qualified as weak and that was something she could not accept.

CHAPTER FOUR

In the early hours of the following morning, Erin rocked her son, Lorcan, on her lap. A nightmare had wakened him and it always took a while to comfort him and soothe him back to sleep.

'Mum…' he framed drowsily, fixing big dark eyes on her as she smoothed his short tousled curls back from his brow, lashes lowering again as tiredness swept him away again.

Much like her son, Erin was utterly exhausted. When she had arrived back at Stanwick to collect her car Sam had wanted a briefing on Cristo's impressions, which had stretched into a meeting that lasted a couple of hours. Sam was keen for his properties to join the Donakis empire because he sincerely believed that a businessman of Cristo's standing could take his three hotels—his life's work—to a higher level. For the first time Erin had felt uncomfortable with the older man, too aware that she was not being entirely honest with him. He didn't know she had had a previous relationship with Cristo Donakis and she did not want him to know. If Sam were to realise that Cristo was the guy who had ditched her and ignored her letters and calls for assistance when she found herself pregnant, he would automatically distrust the younger man. And why should her messy personal life interfere with Sam's plans for retirement? Letting that happen, she felt, would be more wrong than continuing to keep her secrets.

Lorcan shifted against her shoulder, his curly black hair tickling her chin, a warm weight of solid sleeping toddler.

'Tuck him back into bed quickly,' a voice advised quietly from the doorway.

As Deidre Turner, a small blonde woman, moved past to hastily flip back the bedding and assist her daughter in settling the little boy back into his cot, Erin sighed and stood up. 'I'm sorry Lorcan wakened you again.'

'Don't be silly. I don't have to get up as early as you do in the morning,' her mother replied. 'Go back to bed. You look like you're sleepwalking. I don't know what Sam's thinking of, keeping you at work so late. He has no appreciation of the fact that you want to spend time with your family in the evening.'

'Why should he have? He's never had children to worry about,' Erin murmured soothingly, twitching the covers back over her son's small prone body. 'Sam always likes to wind down with a chat at the end of the day and he's very excited about the possibility of selling up.'

'That's all right for him, but if he does sell up where's it going to leave you and the rest of the employees?' Deidre questioned worriedly. 'We couldn't possibly manage on my pension.'

Erin patted her mother's tense shoulder gently. 'We'll survive. Apparently the law protects our jobs in a take-over. But I'll find work somewhere else if need be.'

'It won't be easy with the state the economy's in.

There aren't many jobs out there to find,' the older woman protested.

'We'll be all right,' Erin pronounced with a confidence that she didn't feel and a guilty conscience that she had not felt able to tell her mother that Cristo Donakis was Sam's potential buyer.

But that news would only inflame Deidre Turner, who would also demand to know why her daughter had not made instant use of her access to Cristo to finally tell him that he was a father. In addition her mother was a constant worrier, always in search of the next black cloud on the horizon, and Erin only shared bad news with the older woman if she had no other choice. Checking that her daughter, Nuala, Lorcan's twin sister, was still soundly asleep, curled up in a little round cosy ball inside her cot, Erin returned to bed and lay there in the darkness feeling every bit as anxious as her mother, if not more, as she struggled to count blessings rather than worries.

They lived in a comfortable terraced house. It was rented, not owned. Deidre, predictably imagining less prosperous times ahead, had decided that Erin borrowing money to buy a property for them was far too risky a venture. Her mother's attitude had irritated Erin at the time, but now, with the future danger of unemployment on her mind again she was relieved to be a tenant living in modest accommodation. Sam had reassured her about her job, reminding her that the current legislation would protect his staff with guaranteed employment under the new ownership. But there was often a way round such rules, Erin ruminated worriedly, and, when she was already aware that Cristo didn't want her on his staff, it would only be sensible to immediately begin looking for a new position. Unhappily that might take months to achieve but it was doable, wasn't it? She had to be more positive, stronger, fired up and ready to meet the challenges ahead.

But, Cristo was not a challenge. He was like a great big massive rock set squarely in her path and she didn't know how to get round such an obstacle. He believed she had stolen from him. But why hadn't he pursued that at the time? Why hadn't he called in the police? Erin was thinking back hard, reckoning that by the time Cristo received proof of her supposed theft he would have been married. Had he put the police on her, the fact that she was his ex would soon have emerged and perhaps got into the newspapers. Would that have embarrassed him? She didn't think that the Cristo she recalled would have embarrassed that easily. But that publicity might have embarrassed or annoyed his bride. Was it even possible that Lisandra and Erin had both been in a relationship with Cristo *at the same time*? And that he had feared having that fact exposed? After all, Cristo had got married barely three months after ditching Erin and few couples went from first meeting to marrying that fast. Had he been two-timing both of them? She had never had cause to believe that he was unfaithful to her but refused to believe that he would be incapable of such behaviour. After all, what had she ever really known about Cristo when she had not even suspected that he was about to dump her?

Erin had always liked things safe and certain and she never took risks. The one time she had—Cristo—it had gone badly wrong. On that level she and Cristo were total opposites because nothing thrilled Cristo more than taking a risk or meeting a challenge. So when he had started calling her to ask her out after finally beating her at swimming she had said no, sorry, again and again and again until he had finally manoeuvred her into attending a party at his apartment, urging her to bring friends as her guests.

Her presence bolstered by the presence of Elaine and Tom, it had proved a strangely magical evening with Cristo, she later appreciated, on his very best behaviour. At the end of the night Cristo had kissed her for the first time and that single kiss had been so explosive, it had blown the lid off her wildest dreams…and terrified her. She had known straight off that Cristo Donakis was a high-risk venture: lethally dangerous to her peace of mind.

'I like you…I do like you,' she had told Cristo lamely while still shaking like a leaf in the aftermath of the intense passion that had flared up between them. 'Why can't we just be friends?'

'Friends?' Cristo had echoed as though that word had never come his way before.

'That's what I'd prefer,' she had said brightly.

'I don't do that,' he had told her drily.

With those reservations she'd had more sense at the outset of their affair than she had shown later on, she acknowledged painfully. And once she had had the twins, her life had been turned upside down. She was ashamed to realise that she had been so angry with Cristo in that hotel suite that she had actually been threatening to tell him she was the mother of his children. What aberration had almost driven her to that insane brink? He would not want her children, would never agree to take on the role of father, would only angrily resent the position she put him in and make her feel small and humiliated, a burden he resented. Surely she was entitled to retain some pride when there was no perceptible advantage to telling him the truth?

Cristo had, after all, once confided in her that one of his friends' girlfriends had had a termination. 'It broke them up,' he had commented flatly. 'Few couples survive that sort of stress. I'm not sure I'll ever be ready for children. I prefer my life without baggage.'

And she had got the not exactly subtle message he had taken the trouble to put across, his so clever dark eyes pinned to hers: *Don't do that to me!* Revealingly, it had been the one and only time he ever chose to make her a party to confidential information about someone he knew for Cristo was, by instinct, very discreet. She had taken it as a warning that if she fell pregnant, he would want her to have a termination and their relationship would be over. It still infuriated her that it had actually been entirely his fault that she had conceived and, although she had later grown desperate enough to try and contact him to ask for financial help, she had known even then that the announcement she had to make of his impending fatherhood would infuriate him. Cristo was too arrogant and controlling to appreciate surprises from any source. That a woman could give birth to a baby without a man's prior agreement to accept the responsibility would no doubt strike him as very unfair. No, she saw no point whatsoever in telling Cristo that he was the father of two young children.

Even so, what was she planning to do about his threat to reveal that file of impressive evidence? Cristo was threatening the security of her entire family. Everything she had worked to achieve could vanish overnight. Not only Erin, but her mother and her children would pay the cost of her losing her job and salary. On the other hand, if she could sink her pride enough to play Cristo's cruel game, that file would never see the light of day and at the very least she would have another year of safe employment and plenty of time in which to search for an alternative position. What was one weekend out of the rest of her life, really? She pictured her mother's face earlier, drawn and troubled as she fretted about the hotel group even changing hands. Life had taught Deidre Turner to fear the unknown and the unexpected. She did not deserve to be caught up in the upheaval that was gathering on her daughter's horizon and there was little Erin would not have done to protect her children from the instability she had suffered growing up.

Unhappily, Erin believed that the entire situation was her own fault. Hadn't she ignored everybody's advice in getting involved with Cristo in the first place? Nobody had had a good word to say about Cristo, pointing out that his reputation as a womaniser spoke for him. And why had she made herself even more dependent by agreeing to go and work for him? Was that wise? her friends had asked worriedly. And no, nothing she had done that year with Cristo had been wise. Hadn't she hung on in there even when the going got rough and her lover's lack of commitment was blatantly obvious? He had not even managed to make it back into the UK to celebrate her last birthday with her. She had asked for trouble and now trouble had well and truly come home to roost. Cristo was not going to agree to play nice. Cristo had had over two years to fester over the conviction that she had dared to steal from him. Cristo was out for blood.

* * *

As the sun went down in a blaze of glory, Cristo was staring out at the shaded gardens of his foster parents' much-loved second home away from the smog and heavy traffic in Athens. On his terms, it was homely rather than impressive and it might be situated on the private island of Thesos, which Cristo had inherited at the age of twenty-one, but that was its sole claim to exclusivity.

Vasos and Appollonia Denes had always been extremely scrupulous when it came to enriching themselves in any way through their custodianship of a very wealthy little boy. Both his parents saw life in black and white with no shades of grey, which made them difficult to deal with, Cristo reflected in intense frustration. He had spent three very trying days locked in an office with Vasos, struggling to pull his father's company back from the edge of bankruptcy without the escape route of even being able to offer the firm a cheap loan. They would not touch his money in any form. Yet his father was suffering from so much stress that he had fallen asleep in the middle of dinner and his mother was still worryingly quiet and troubled, in spite of all her protestations to the contrary. She had never quite recovered from the nervous breakdown she had gone through eighteen months earlier.

Had they had any idea what he was engaged in with Erin Turner they would have been sincerely appalled, Cristo acknowledged grudgingly. They adored him, always thought the best of him, and firmly believed that with the conservative upbringing they had given him he must have absorbed their values, their decent principles. But even as a child Cristo had understood what it took to please his parents and he had learned how to pretend as well as accept that it wasn't always within his power to cure the evils of the world for them… His lean strong face hardened fiercely as a particularly unpleasant instance of that impossibility twanged deep in his conscience. He poured himself another drink and shook the memory off again fast.

When life was full of eighteen-hour days and the constant demands of his business empire, Erin was a wonderful distraction to toy with, that was *all*. If she didn't phone him within the next twenty-four hours, however, they would be entering round two of their battle of wits and he would play hardball. He was already figuring out his next move, no regrets whatsoever. Plainly he lacked the forgiving gene. That was becoming obvious even to him and he was not a man given to self-examination. But the lust driving him was on another plane altogether. One kiss…hell, what was he, a teenager to have got so hot and bothered?

And why did it disturb him that right this very minute she might be lying in a bed with Sam Morton, ensuring his continuing devotion in the easiest and most basic way a woman could? Why should that matter to him? Why, in fact, did that mental vision make him seethe? It should turn him off, douse the fire she roused…*disgust* him. But all Cristo could think about just then, indeed the only blindingly blue stretch of sky in his immediate future, was the prospect of that weekend. A weekend of the most perfect fantasy. Of course, it went without saying that fantasy would inevitably turn out to be dross, he pondered cynically. And then it would be over and he would be cured of this inconvenient, incomprehensible craving for her cheating little carcass for all time.

Done and dusted. He savoured that ideal prospect, increasingly keen to reach that moment of equilibrium.

Erin picked up the phone, her blood solidifying like ice in her veins. Caving in *hurt;* it was something she didn't do any more. Show weakness and people often fell on you like vultures. She was not the woman she had been three years earlier. But while she might be tougher, it was useless because Cristo had put her in the no-win corner, giving her no choice other than to try and protect those that she loved by whatever means were within her power.

'Yes, Miss Turner,' some faceless PA trilled at the end of the line. 'Mr Donakis mentioned that you would be calling. I'll put you through.'

His sheer certainty that she would surrender struck another blow to her already battered pride while she thought painfully of all the other times she had tried to speak to Cristo two and a half years earlier and had run into an endless brick wall of refusals. Of course, a call from an ex would not have been welcome to a newly engaged male but the potential offer of sex, it seemed, occupied a whole other plane of acceptability.

'Erin,' Cristo drawled smoothly. 'How may I help you?'

'Will the weekend of the fifth suit?' Her voice was breathless with strain and something very like anguish was rising inside her, for she had lost control of the situation. In the back of her mind something was shrieking that she just could not be doing this, could not possibly be contemplating such a sleazy arrangement, but her brain was mercifully in control as she pictured her children and her mother and once again acknowledged what was most important.

'That's two weeks away,' Cristo growled.

'And it's the soonest I can manage,' Erin said as coolly as if it were a business appointment she was setting up.

'Agreed. Someone will be in touch about the arrangements. Have a current passport available.'

'Why? Where on earth are you planning to go?' she gasped.

'Somewhere discreet. I'll see you on the fifth,' he murmured, the guarded quality in his tone letting her know that he was not alone.

Dry-mouthed, she replaced the phone, pure hatred strong and immovable as a concrete block forming inside her. What had she ever done to him that he should seek her out and threaten to destroy her life? So, he thought she was a thief. *Get over it*, she wanted to shriek at him. When they had been together she had refused to accept expensive gifts and clothes from him—did that telling fact count for nothing? In every way possible she had tried to make their relationship one of equals and her mind slid back into the past…

Surprisingly, he had banished her reluctance to enter a relationship with him with the use of romantic gestures. He had sent her flowers, occasional witty texts to keep her up to date with his life and on Valentine's Day he had sent her the most exquisite card and invited her out to dinner again. As there had not been a glimmer of him showing any interest in any other female during that period, Erin didn't know a woman alive who would have not succumbed to so persuasive an onslaught from a very handsome male. So, she had finally gone out with him, just the two of them, thoroughly enjoyed herself and that was how it had begun: date after date but just kissing, nothing more because she wouldn't agree to anything more. And, no fan of the celibate life, Cristo had protested, persisting with his need for an explanation until she finally admitted that he would be her first lover. Disconcerted by that admission, he had surprised her by agreeing to wait until *she* felt that the moment was right and she had loved him all the more for not putting pressure on her.

And in the end she had slept with him because she couldn't say no to her own craving any longer and the experience, the connection she had felt with him from the outset of true intimacy, had been unutterably wonderful. Four months into their affair, probably tiring of the number of times she was not available through work or the extra hours she put in as a personal trainer to a few select clients, he had offered her the job of manager at the Mobila spa in his flagship London hotel. She had thought long and hard before she accepted but as she was already working as a deputy manager she had believed that the position was well within her capabilities. She had been more afraid that working for Cristo might change their relationship but it had not occurred to her that her new colleagues might resent her inescapably personal ties to their employer.

At the time she had been taking the contraceptive pill but, in spite of trying several different brands, she had suffered mood changes that made her feel like a stranger inside her own skin. Ultimately, Cristo had suggested that he take care of precautions and soon after had come that disturbing little chat about the friend's girlfriend, who had had a termination, that same possibility obviously having awakened Cristo's concern on his own account. After six months she had virtually lived in Cristo's apartment when he was there and he had begun asking her to join him on his travels. She had pointed out that she couldn't just walk out on her job and expect her staff to take her seriously. He had understood that but he hadn't *liked* it and around the same time he had started to question the amount of time she spent with Tom while he was abroad. Tom Harcourt was the closest thing Erin had ever had to a brother. They had met on the same university course and had stayed close friends when Tom also found work in London. There had never been a sexual spark between Erin and Tom but they got on like a house on fire, something Cristo had witnessed on several occasions and had evidently resented or found suspicious. Eight months into their relationship Cristo and Erin had had a huge, horrible row about Tom and Erin had stormed home in a temper.

'How would you like it if I had a female friend that close?' Cristo had demanded.

And in truth she wouldn't have liked it at all, but she loved Tom like a brother and refused to give him up.

'You're too possessive for me,' she had told Cristo, inflaming him as he furiously denied the charge.

'You're a very beautiful woman—Tom has to be aware of that. Truly platonic relationships don't exist,' Cristo had insisted. 'One party or the other always feels something more.'

'Either you trust me or you don't,' Erin had reasoned, stripping the dispute back to the bare bones while resisting the dangerous temptation to inform him that he had a shockingly jealous streak.

'Cristo is in love with you,' her more experienced

flatmate, Elaine, had pronounced with amusement. 'I didn't think it would happen but in my opinion men only get that possessive when they're keen.'

And that heartening forecast was why Erin had extended an olive branch to Cristo after a two-week silence while they both smouldered after that argument. In any case, by that stage Tom was already taking a back seat in her life because he had met the woman, Melissa, whom he would eventually marry. She had then waited hopefully for Cristo to demonstrate a more serious attitude towards her but it had never happened. They had spent Christmas and even his birthday apart while he went home to Greece without even dropping a hint that he might consider asking her to accompany him. Only one element of their affair had stayed the same: his passion for her body had never ebbed right to the very last night they had ever spent together and that same night was the one during which she was convinced she had fallen pregnant.

One week later, after bailing on her birthday party at his hotel, he had dumped her. He had had no qualms about the way he did it either, for he had walked into the spa, asked for a moment alone with her in her office and strolled away five minutes later, the deed done.

'You and I?' he had said drily. 'We've run our course and I'd like to move on.'

And he had moved on at supersonic speed to a wife, Erin recalled, settling back into the present with a dazed look on her delicate face. What she couldn't grasp was why, after that emotion-free affront of a dismissal almost three years ago, he should want to revisit the past. It didn't make sense to her. Yes, he might want to punish her for supposedly thieving from him, but how did the act of sex, anything but retribution with a guy like Cristo Donakis, encompass that ambition?

CHAPTER FIVE

Two weeks later, Erin stepped out of the car that had collected her at the airport and breathed in slow and deep. Italy, Tuscany in fact, not at all the setting that she had dimly expected Cristo to provide. In truth she had assumed the weekend would take place in London at his apartment, if he still lived there in the city, or even in one of his hotels. A grand fortified house presiding over an incredibly scenic hidden Italian valley had not featured at all.

Even with the sun starting to set in a golden blaze, the views of grape terraces, arrow-shaped cypresses, pine-forested slopes and silver-grey olive trees were magnificent; almost as much so as the wide graceful house with its shallow terracotta red roof and twin lines of tall elegant windows. Bells tinkled while sheep grazed on stretches of lush green grass in a timeless pastoral scene. It was not the backdrop she would have given to Cristo, whom she had once believed could only thrive on the often insane pace of city life.

A small balding manservant was already grasping the small case she had travelled with and with an expansive wave of one hand he welcomed her in English, introduced himself as Vincenzo and invited her to follow him indoors to an imposing marble hall that echoed with their footsteps. He escorted her straight up the sweeping marble staircase to a beautifully furnished bedroom decorated in masculine shades of gold and green. Her cheeks flared as she gazed at the wide gold-draped bed and hastily she glanced away again, preceding Vincenzo into the superb modern bathroom and politely smiling in admiration.

Did the wretched man know what she was here for? Or did he simply assume that she was yet another one of Cristo's women? And whatever he thought, what did it matter? She studied her taut reflection with self-loathing. Get over yourself, she told herself urgently. It might feel like a lifetime since she had had sex but at the end of the day sex was just sex even with Cristo and not worth risking her security over. She was being practical, choosing the safest option...

Over the past two weeks negotiations over the buyout of Sam's hotels had speeded up to reach agreement. The deal was signed, sealed and delivered and, whether she liked it or not, she was going to be working for Cristo Donakis again, although presumably only after that forensic accounting team he had mentioned had convinced him that she was to be trusted after all. The sting of his conviction that she was a thief still lingered though, not to mention the necessity of having had to lie outright to her trusting mother to travel to Italy. That latter act sat like a giant stone on her conscience.

Her face and her heart troubled, Erin doffed her light raincoat and agreed to come downstairs to enjoy the coffee that Vincenzo was offering. She had told her mother that she was catching the train up to Scotland to stay with Tom and his wife, Melissa, and their new baby, Karen. What else could she have told the older woman? Deidre Turner would have had a heart attack had she known the truth of what her wayward daughter was about to do and guilt nagged at Erin. Surely sometimes a lie was kinder than the truth, she reasoned uncertainly. But that was of little comfort to a young woman raised to 'tell the truth and shame the devil'.

Coffee was served on the terrace in the warmth of early evening and she thought about Lorcan and Nuala, resenting the loss of a weekend that she had expected to spend with her twins. As she abstractedly took in the fabulous view shadowing into dark hills and tree tops her phone buzzed and she drew it from her bag.

Wear your hair loose, the text told her.

Cristo was reducing her to the level of a toy with a starring role in *his* fantasy. The taste of her coffee soured in her mouth. She was sick with nerves. Cristophe Donakis was the man she had once loved beyond belief. Although she had worked hard to hide it, she had absolutely adored him and their intimacy had only added another dimension to that love. This demeaning emotion-free encounter would destroy even the good memories. Though perhaps that would be a godsend? Was Cristo getting a kick out of having her at his disposal? Cristo enjoyed power. Teeth gritting, she finished the coffee and went back upstairs to change. Was she supposed to dress as if this were a date or await his arrival in that vast bed? Tears stung her eyes and she blinked them away furiously as she headed for a shower. No, absolutely no way was she going to wait in the bed! Swathed in a towel, she tugged a silky blue dress from her case.

Cristo leapt out of the helicopter and strode up to the

villa, impatience and hunger burning through him. He hadn't been worth a damn all day, all week for that matter! Just the thought of Erin being there had wiped out his wits, Vincenzo's call to confirm her arrival catching him in the middle of a board meeting. How many times had he told himself he shouldn't be doing this? What the hell, he reasoned furiously, why shouldn't he be a bastard for a change? He had let her off the hook too lightly three years ago. This— being with her one more time—was an indulgence but it was also an exorcism, and when it was done he would be done with her as well.

The pulse in Erin's neck was beating like crazy as she hovered by the bedroom window, refusing to look outside while her tummy twisted into knots. She had heard the helicopter landing, knew Cristo liked to fly himself, and knew it would be him and that within minutes he would walk through the bedroom door. She clasped her hands tightly together, willing back her nerves, striving for calm and cool.

And then the door flew open, rocking back on its hinges to frame Cristo, brilliant black diamond eyes snaking across the room to rest on her, his tall well-built body casting a long shadow in the lamp light. And there she was, silvery pale hair tumbling round her shoulders, something pretty and blue swirling round her petite little body, *waiting* for him just as he remembered from times gone by. *Erin*. He savoured her, noting the glow of self-consciousness that coloured the beautiful delicacy of her features. He experienced such a charge of hunger at the first glance that a predatory smile crossed his mobile male mouth.

'Cristo…' Erin contrived to enunciate with admira-

ble clarity, only the breathy quietness of her voice letting her down.

'Erin,' he breathed thickly, closing the distance between them and hauling her straight into his arms.

He said something in Greek as he gazed down at
her and she would have given anything to know what
it was. 'What—?'

'Don't want to talk, *koukla mou,*' Cristo husked, his
breath fanning her cheek as he bent his handsome dark
head.

His eyes, those beautiful beautiful eyes, lion gold
surrounded by spiky black lashes, held hers fast and she
literally stopped breathing because the clean designer
scent of him was drenching her with every mouthful
of air. He looked so good, so irretrievably, undeniably
good that his pure impact overwhelmed her. He kissed
the corner of her mouth in a tiny teasing caress and
she shivered, her thoughts blanking out, her body taking over and she wanted more, wanted more so badly
that it hurt. His mouth found hers with a sudden urgency that she welcomed. Her tongue slid against his
and the pressure of his lips increased in a deep hot kiss
that blew her away. In the midst of it he wrenched free
of his jacket and dropped it, yanked at his tie and she
trailed it free, her fingers releasing the shirt button at
his strong brown throat.

And it took no thought to do any of those things and
she was shaken by the instinct driving her at a level
she didn't understand. Her fingers curved to one high
cheekbone as she struggled to stay upright with her
heart slamming against her breastbone as hard as though
she were in race. Her legs felt weak, insufficient to support her and she was fiercely aware of the empty ache

in her pelvis and the swelling tightness of her breasts as he spread his big hands over her buttocks and crushed her into his hard erection.

'I'm burning alive for you,' Cristo growled almost accusingly, spinning her round to find the zip on her dress and taking care of it with efficiency.

'Me too,' Erin admitted with a bitterness she couldn't hide, her whole body throbbing with uncontrollable desire as deft fingers brushed the straps of her dress off her slight shoulders and the garment pooled in a silky heap round her feet.

Breathing audibly, Cristo spun her back to him and bent to curve his hands round her slim thighs, hitching her up against him and bringing her down on the bed with a sound of satisfaction that started deep in his broad chest. It's just sex, *amazing* sex, he adjusted helplessly, but the burn, the burn of excitement was indescribable. He slid a hand beneath her to unclasp her bra and stared down into her amethyst eyes, purple blue like precious gems. Thief, he told himself, liar, *cheat* but that little mantra of reminders didn't work its desired magic. He ripped off his shirt, felt her hands sweeping up, up over his chest and honestly wondered if he could hold it together long enough to get inside her.

'How can you still do this to me?' he demanded in a fierce undertone, shimmering hot golden eyes pinned to the flushed triangle of her face and then sinking down a level to concentrate on the pale breasts he had uncovered, firm little mounds adorned with large pink nipples that magnetised his attention.

Claiming a straining bud with his mouth, Cristo suckled strongly, using his hands, his lips and the edge of his teeth because he knew how sensitive she was there. As her slim length jackknifed under him, spine arching on a strangled moan, his sense of achievement increased and he let his lips rove hungrily over her dainty breasts, lingering on the swollen straining peaks to torment them with pleasure. His attention glued to her prone body, he backed off the bed again and unzipped his trousers.

Her face hot pink with shame and discomfiture, Erin sat up and clasped her knees. She didn't want to enjoy anything they did. She wanted to lie there like a stone statue and stay inwardly untouched and detached from him. But Cristo was far too expert a lover to allow her that kind of escape route and he was seducing a response out of her resistant body.

'I didn't intend to fall on you like a wild animal the minute I came through the door,' he volunteered impatiently. 'I was planning on having dinner first.'

Erin averted her gaze, the victim of unwelcome memories of a passion that had never gone off the boil. 'You were never very good at waiting. It was always like this for us—'

'There is no "us" any more.'

Erin lowered her lashes. He was wrong. Lorcan and Nuala were a wonderful combination of their respective genes and unless she was very much mistaken her toddlers had inherited his volatile nature. Lorcan was wilful and hot-tempered and Nuala was sharp as paint and mercurial, neither of them demonstrating an iota of their mother's quieter, more settled personality. But she was grateful that Cristo didn't know about them. Lorcan and Nuala would never get the chance to emulate their father's tough cynical outlook on the world, where what he wanted always came ahead of what was best for other people. He would not get the chance to turn them into spoilt, selfish children and, after the manner in which he had corralled her back into his bed, she refused to feel guilty about the fact.

She glanced up in the silence.

'You look like you're plotting,' Cristo remarked thoughtfully.

He towered over her, naked and aroused, gazing down at her with hot golden eyes of appreciation. She was appalled when her body reacted deep down inside, her nipples tingling as dampness formed at the heart of her.

'What on earth would I be plotting?'

'I don't know.' He stroked the tight set of her sultry mouth with a considering fingertip. 'But you're wearing the same face you wore when you found out I'd taken business associates to a lap-dancing club, *koukla mou*.'

Erin flushed as he came down beside her. 'Not one of my better memories.'

Cristo unclasped the hands she had tightened round her knees and pulled her back against his warm, hair-roughened torso. 'Nor mine, but unfortunately that kind of venue is par for the course with certain men.'

Her breath scissored in her throat as he found her breasts again, gently, surely shaping and tugging at the swollen tips. He pressed her back against the pillows, long brown fingers dipping below the waistband of her knickers, moving across bare smooth skin to stroke her clitoris. As the ache between her thighs intensified, she shut her eyes tight. He kissed her with hot driving force, skimmed off that last garment and pressed his lips to the smooth slope of her belly. Her eyes flew wide because she had silvery stretchmarks there from her pregnancy and she quivered as he trailed his expert mouth over her abdomen and then lower, startling her with that move. He found her with his mouth and his fingers, delving into the honeyed heat of her until she moaned, hips squirming as the pleasure built. He tipped her back, drowning her in sweet sensation that sent her out of control. Her breath sounded in audible gasps as she shifted helplessly up to him, wanting, *needing* and then response took over to send her racing into an explosive climax.

'I love watching you come…it must be the only time in your life that you let go of control,' Cristo husked, looking down at her with an unusually reflective light in his keen gaze. 'You're so different from me.'

Emerging dizzily from the tremors of ecstasy still rocking her body, Erin looked up into his lean dark face and the stunning eyes engaged in tracking her every change of expression. She felt exposed, vulnerable, shaken that he had already seduced her so thoroughly that she could barely recall what day it was, never mind how they had ended up in a bed at such indecent speed. 'I don't want to be here doing this with you,' she said fiercely.

'Liar.' He brought his mouth down on hers and her tongue slid against his again and that single kiss was so passionate she shivered.

Cristo donned a condom and came over her like a one-man invasion force, tipping her legs over his shoulders and driving into her so hard and deep that her head fell back in a curtain of shiny silver blonde hair, neck arching feverishly in reaction. It was good, hell it was *amazing*, she thought furiously, angry with herself, enraged that she hadn't found it possible to lie there without responding and destroy his desire for her. She knew him well enough to know that if she had held back and failed to respond he wouldn't have persisted. He shifted position and ground into her faster with hungry pounding strokes that made her heart race as though she were in a marathon. He groaned with unashamed pleasure as she cried out, bucking up to him, reacting helplessly to the delicious friction of his fluid rhythm. And she felt the heat mushrooming up from her pelvis again until an explosion of light shot through her like a flash of white-hot fire, shooting wild hot tension along every limb. He pulsed inside her and groaned as she came apart at the seams in another shattering orgasm.

By the time she came free of that shattering onslaught of raw pleasure, she was trembling and, surprisingly, he still had his arms round her, one hand splayed across her stomach as he pressed his sensual mouth to her damp cheek. 'You're amazing. That was *so* worth waiting for, *koukla mou*.'

But she hadn't made him wait; they had ended up in bed five minutes after his arrival. *I'm easy*, she decided painfully, marvelling that she was still lying in his arms and revelling in that unbelievable sense of closeness with him again. How could she possibly feel connected to Cristophe Donakis again? It felt as if almost three years had vanished in a time slip to deposit her back to when she had cherished such private and vulnerable moments with the man she loved. Only she didn't love him any more, she told herself bitterly, and he had never loved her and, what was more, he had ruthlessly blackmailed her back into his bed. As she began to reclaim her wits and pull away Cristo pulled away from her to disappear into the bathroom.

She listened to the shower running and wondered how she would live with the victory she had given him, how she would ever look in the mirror and like herself again. It was all right to tell herself that she had done what she had to do to protect her life and her children's, but what she had just allowed to happen went against her every principle. It was a punishment to appreciate that she had participated in and enjoyed her own downfall.

Lithe, bronzed and truly magnificent, Cristo reappeared with a towel wrapped round his lean hips just as a knock sounded on the bedroom door. 'I told Vincenzo to bring up dinner,' he remarked carelessly.

Erin scrambled out of bed naked and vanished into the bathroom to use the shower. She was on automatic pilot, desperate to escape his presence lest she lose what little distance she had contrived to achieve. Stepping out of the shower again, she saw the black towelling robe hanging on the back of the door and made use of it because she hadn't packed anything that practical. She rolled up the sleeves, tied the sash tight.

Cristo had donned close-fitting jeans and a black tee. A heated trolley now stood beside the small table in the corner.

'How did Vincenzo get all that food up here?' she asked stiffly.

'There's a lift. The last owner was an elderly lady with mobility problems.'

'When did you buy this place?'

'About a year ago. I wanted somewhere to relax between business trips,' Cristo said, sounding amazingly calm and distant after what they had just shared. 'What would you like to eat?'

'I'll see to myself.' Her tummy rumbled as, maintaining a scrupulous distance from his lean, powerful body, she studied the tempting array of dishes. She was surprised that she was so hungry but then nervous tension had pretty much killed her appetite over the previous forty-eight hours while she was forced to pretend to everyone around her that life was normal. She chose meat-stuffed *tortelloni* and *Panzanella* salad and lifted a slice of home baked bread.

His lean, darkly handsome face composed, Cristo poured wine for them both and sat down in a fluid movement. His assurance set her teeth on edge. He had blasted her pride and confidence out of existence because all of a sudden she didn't know who she was any more. She was not the mature, self-contained woman she had believed she was and that acknowledgement hurt.

'Doesn't it bother you that you blackmailed me into bed?' Erin shot at him abruptly.

'It might have started out that way, but that's not how it concluded,' Cristo fielded smooth as glass, his gaze welded to her. Gleaming silvery fair hair tumbled loose round her slight shoulders, accentuating her flawless features. He had burned for her from the first moment he saw her standing wet and tousled beside the swimming pool where they had met. He had burned the same way when he met her again in Sam Morton's office. He wasn't happy that she set him on fire. He wasn't happy that one wildly exciting taste of her had only primed him to want the next. *Toxic,* he reminded himself grimly.

Erin met cool, measuring, dark golden eyes that contained not an ounce of remorse and gritted her teeth, afraid to utter a word in her own defence, for what exactly could she say? They both knew that she had not

played the part of an unwilling victim. 'I don't understand why you wanted me here,' she admitted tightly.
'After all, when we split up, you made it clear that you
were bored with our relationship.'

Cristo became very still. 'I never said I was bored.'

Barely forgotten frustration invaded Erin afresh. It
was a throwback to the bewilderment of the past when
she had tormented herself for months in the aftermath
of their breakup wondering what she had done or not
done to make him want his freedom back. Suddenly
that old curiosity was biting into her like a knife point.
'Then why did you ditch me?'

His lean, strong face was impassive. 'I doubt that you
want the answer to that question.'

Erin stabbed a piece of juicy tomato with her fork.
'It's a long time ago, Cristo,' she said drily.

'Precisely,' he slotted in sardonically.

'But I would *still* like to know why,' Erin completed
doggedly.

Cristo set down his wine glass, brilliant dark eyes
pinned to her and she felt the chill like ice water spill-
ing across her skin. 'You cheated on me...'

Erin stared back at him in astonishment. 'No. I
didn't.'

'I caught the guy in your bed in your hotel room the
night after your birthday bash,' Cristo countered flatly.
'You cheated on me.'

Erin was frowning. 'Who did you see in my hotel
room?'

Cristo shrugged a broad shoulder and dealt her a sa-
tiric glance. 'I have no idea who he was. I let myself
into the room intending to surprise you and instead *I*
got the surprise.'

Erin was stunned. 'But I wasn't there—you didn't see me.'

Cristo dealt her a scornful look. 'I saw the man, the discarded clothes, the wine glasses and I could hear the shower running in the bathroom. I didn't need to see you as well.'

Erin was so tense she was barely breathing. In a sudden movement she pushed back her chair and stood upright, her amethyst eyes bright with anger. 'Well, actually you did because that *wasn't* me in the bathroom! I didn't even stay in London that night.'

Cristo gave her an unimpressed look. 'It was your room and he was in your bed—'

Anger coursed through her in a torrent of incredulous rage. 'And you're only telling me this now, nearly three *years* later? Why didn't you mention it at the time?'

'I didn't see any point in staging a messy confrontation. I had seen all I needed to see,' Cristo derided with harsh assurance.

CHAPTER SIX

ERIN genuinely wanted to strangle Cristo at that moment. In the space of seconds she was reviewing the misery she had endured after their parting and finally grasping why he had dumped her with so little fanfare. Hostility at his latest misjudgement roared through her, her facial bones drawing taut below her fine skin. 'You had seen all you needed to see—is that a fact?' she snapped back furiously.

An ebony brow elevated with sardonic cool. 'What more evidence would I have required?'

'*Proper* evidence!' Erin fired back at him quick as a flash with more than a hint of his own intensity. 'Because that wasn't me in that bathroom. I didn't stay in London that night. I got a call from the hospital to tell me that my mother had been rushed to Casualty with a suspected heart attack. Tom and his girlfriend offered to run me home—Tom's kid brother, Dennis, asked if he could use my hotel room to stay in town with his girlfriend. I said yes, why wouldn't I have? I wasn't expecting you to turn up. When you told me you couldn't make it home to my party, you also said that you probably wouldn't make it back to London for at least another twenty-four hours.'

His darkly handsome features set like stone, Cristo gave her an unyielding look. 'I don't believe your explanation.'

At that inflammatory admission, Erin simply grabbed up the bottle of wine and poured it over his head, watching with satisfaction as the golden liquid cascaded down over his black hair and granite-hard masculine features. Startled by the assault, he leapt up with an irate Greek curse and wrenched the bottle from her grasp. 'Have you gone insane?' he raked back at her in ringing disbelief.

Untouched by any form of guilt, Erin grimly watched him dry his face with a napkin. 'I must've been when I got involved with you. How dare you assume that I slept with some other guy? How dare you just accept that and judge me for it? After the amount of time I was with you, I deserved more respect. How could you condemn me without a hearing?'

'I'm not having this conversation with you—I'm going for a second shower,' Cristo declared, striding towards the bathroom door.

Erin moved liked lightning to get there ahead of him and leant back in the doorway, daring him to shift her out of his path. 'You are so stubborn. But I could put my hand on a bible and *swear* that I wasn't in the Mobila hotel that night.'

'You were there!' Cristo breathed rawly, wrathful challenge scored into every hard angle and hollow of his breathtakingly handsome face.

'No, I wasn't!' Erin snapped back at him angrily. 'How could you even credit that I'd spent the night with another man?'

'Why not? I couldn't make it back in time for your birth-day party and I knew you had to be furious with me—'

'Not so furious that I would have got into bed with someone else! I can't believe that you thought that of me and just walked away from it.'

His eyes hostile, his hard jaw line squared and he said nothing.

'Of course, I understand why now,' Erin continued thinly. 'You are so full of ego and pride. Walking away was the easiest thing to do—'

'That's not why I said nothing,' Cristo argued, his Greek accent roughening every vowel sound, anger glittering in the golden blaze of his eyes. 'I had had doubts about you for a while. There had been other…things that made me suspicious—'

'Name them,' she challenged.

'I will not discuss them with you—'

'You unreasonable, *arrogant*…' she slammed back, so enraged with him that she was trembling. 'In all the time we were together I never so much as looked at an-other man but that wasn't good enough for you, was it? You're jealous and possessive to the bone—you couldn't even stand me spending time with Tom!'

Eyes glowing like the heart of a fire between black spiky lashes, Cristo closed his hands to her waist and lifted her off her feet to set her to one side. 'I've told you. We're not having this discussion.'

Erin followed him into the bathroom. 'We definitely are, Cristo. You can't accuse me of infidelity and expect me to accept it in silence! What's wrong with you? You think I'm a thief as well but you said nothing about that either at the time. In retrospect don't you find all this muck being flung at me a little strange?'

Cristo was engaged in stripping off his wine-stained clothing. 'In what way strange?' he queried curtly.

'It's beginning to look to me like someone set out to deliberately discredit me in your eyes.'

His handsome mouth took on a sardonic curve as he peeled off his jeans and left them in a heap. 'That sounds like paranoia.'

Erin averted her attention as he stripped off his boxers and discovered that she was studying his long, powerful, hair-roughened thighs instead. The colour in her cheeks heightened as she lifted her head again, struggling to blot out the sight of the lean ropes of muscle banding his powerful torso. 'There's nothing paranoid about my suspicions—'

'You cheated on me and I found out…get over it,' Cristo advised witheringly as he switched on the shower and stepped in, utterly unconcerned by the nudity of his lean bronzed body. But then he had never been shy. 'It's ancient history. Don't try to resurrect it.'

'I wish I'd hit you with that bottle.'

Cristo rammed back the shower door and rested cold dark eyes of warning on her angry, defiant face. 'Don't you ever do anything like that again or I won't be responsible for what I do.'

Erin clashed with scorching golden eyes and her tummy lurched. Rage washed over her again because butterflies were leaping in her pelvis. Infuriatingly her body was reacting to him with all the control of an infatuated adolescent. 'I wish I had cheated on you…the way you treated me, I might as well have done!'

She stalked out of the bathroom. He had knocked her for six with that accusation. He had also taught her that she didn't know him as well as she had always believed she did. Although she had recognised his reserve she had never dreamt that he might have the capacity to keep such big secrets from her. What else didn't she know about Cristo? And what else had happened that had caused him to doubt her loyalty? What were those other 'things' he had grudgingly mentioned? Yanking the bedspread off the bed, and lifting a pillow, she made up the sofa on the far side of the room for her occupation.

'You're not sleeping over there,' Cristo told her tautly.

'I'm certainly not getting back into a bed with a man who thinks I'm a slut as well as a thief!' Erin replied with spirit, pale hair bouncing on her shoulders as she spun round to face him.

Stark naked, Cristo was hauling fresh clothing from drawers. He shot her a censorious appraisal from brilliant dark eyes. 'We have a deal—'

'But I intend to add my own conditions,' Erin declared thinly. 'I'll keep to our agreement *if*—'

'Too late—we already have a deal.'

'If that's your attitude I'm sleeping on the sofa.'

His thick sooty lashes lowered on stunning golden eyes while he surveyed her. 'Do you cheat at cards too?'

'You ought to know—you taught me to play,' she reminded him.

The silence buzzed like an angry wasp. Cristo continued to watch her, his attention locked to the sultry pink pout of her mouth. He wished he had kept his own shut and could not think why he had admitted that he knew of her betrayal. Everything had been going so well until she decided that honour demanded she now prove that she was pure as the driven snow. In exasperation he scored long brown fingers through his damp black hair. 'What conditions?' he demanded impatiently.

'I'll get back into that bed if—and only *if*—you agree to talk to Tom, who will verify that he passed the key card for the room to his brother and later dropped me off at the hospital a hundred miles away to be with my mother.'

Cristo looked pained. 'That's ridiculous.'

Erin tilted her chin. 'No, it's the least of what you owe me.'

'I owe you nothing.' He was poised there insolently, still half naked but for the jeans he had pulled on. Just looking at Cristo made her heartbeat pick up speed and her breathing quicken: he was so physically gorgeous. White-hot sex appeal was bred into his very bones. Even more disturbingly, the wilful line of his beautiful mouth was remarkably like her son, Lorcan's, she registered in dismay, rushing to suppress that unnerving sense of familiarity. Inside himself Cristo was seething with anger, she *did* know that, but Cristo rarely revealed anger on the surface, deeming that a weakness. And one thing Cristophe Donakis did not do was weakness.

'I deserve that you check out my side of the story,' Erin proclaimed as regally as a queen. 'You didn't give me the opportunity three years ago, so the least you can do is take care of the omission now.'

A winged ebony brow quirked. 'And if I agree, you'll get back into bed?'

'I have just one more thing to say.'

'You're pricing yourself out of the market.'

Erin gazed back at him, remembering when she had loved him, when she had simply lived for his quick easy smile and attention and shrinking from the recollection, fearful of ever laying her heart out again. 'No, I'm worth waiting for.'

Cristo dealt her a hungry appraisal that made her triangular face burn as though he had turned an open flame on her skin. 'Speak…'

'Ask yourself why I would commit fraud and put myself at risk of a prison sentence while refusing to accept the valuable diamond jewellery you tried to give me on several occasions,' she advised softly. 'If I wanted money that badly, keeping the diamonds and selling them would have been much more sensible.'

Cristo held her eyes coolly without reaction and then released his breath on a slow measured hiss. 'Get back in bed,' he breathed.

Erin retrieved her pillow and undid the tie on the robe, letting it fall as she scrambled onto the divan. Cristo watched, desire igniting almost simultaneously to raise his temperature. Surely there had never been any woman with paler, more perfect skin or more delicate yet highly feminine curves? He lay down on the bed beside her with a sense that all was right in his world for the first time in a long time. Erin studied the stark beauty of his features, knowing why no other man had tempted her, knowing why she was still heart whole. Nobody had ever come close to comparing to Cristo either in looks or passion. Eyes drowsy, she lifted a hand in the simmering silence and with her forefinger gently traced the volatile curve of his full lower lip. His gaze smouldered and his hand came up to entrap hers, long fingers wrapping round her smaller hand with precision.

'Go to sleep,' he breathed ruefully, noting the shadows that lay below her eyes like bruises. 'You're exhausted.'

Why should it bother him that she looked so tired? Why had he even noticed? His expressive mouth tightened. They were enjoying the equivalent of a two-night stand: finer feelings of any kind were not required. Nor had he any intention of getting caught up in discussing their previous relationship. There was nothing to discuss. But Erin had looked so shocked when he accused her of cheating on him. Perhaps she had been shocked that he had found her out. Clearly her partner that night had stayed silent about Cristo's entry to the hotel room. And Erin had always had a talent for playing innocent and naïve. Once that had charmed him, fooled him. Now it merely set his teeth on edge with suspicion.

What was Erin hoping to get out of this weekend? She was a survivor. As was he and he didn't like the fact that he was enjoying her company so much.

The next day they had breakfast on the terrace midmorning. Erin had slept so late she was embarrassed. Sleeping in, after all, was a luxury she no longer enjoyed at home. The twins woke up at the crack of dawn demanding attention and since their birth Erin had learned to get by on short rations of sleep. Casually garbed in white cotton trousers teamed with a colourful silk top, she spread honey on her toast and enjoyed the picturesque landscape of rolling hills covered with mature chestnut and oak woods at the rear of the villa. It occurred to her that she might as well have been on a pleasure trip, for the accommodation and food were superb and even the company was acceptable.

Acceptable, jeered a little mocking voice in her head as she glanced at Cristo, lean and darkly magnificent in a black polo shirt and tailored chinos, predictably pacing the terrace as he ate and drank, the restive spirit that drove him unable to keep the lid on his sheer energy this early in the day. He had let her sleep undisturbed, had already been up and dressed when he finally wakened her. As his spectacular dark golden eyes surged her she went pink, something akin to panic assailing her as she felt her treacherous body's instant response to his powerful masculinity. There was an ache at the heart of her, a physical reminder of the wild passion they had shared. Yes, *shared*, she labelled, refusing to overlook her own behaviour. The sleazy weekend of her worst imaginings had come nowhere near reality and it had also proved surprisingly informative, she acknowledged wryly as she continued to think deeply about Cristo's admission that he had believed she had cheated on him. How could he not have confronted her about that? And yet she knew why not, she understood the bone-deep unforgiving pride that was so much a part of his nature. He had successfully hidden his anger from her at the time, refusing to vent it, something she could not have done in his place. He had accepted her supposed betrayal and, even now, his lack of faith in her when she had loved him appalled her. As Cristo had reminded her, though, it was the past and she thought it was wiser not to dwell on it.

He took her out for a drive in an open-topped sports car. Such freedom felt strange to her. She was accustomed to taking the twins to the park on Saturday mornings. Guilt weighed her down for she knew that her children would be missing out on that outing because Erin's mother found it difficult to watch over her grandchildren alone in a public place. Lorcan loved to explore and he wandered off, often followed by his sister. Erin had twice found her son standing up to his knees in the boating lake and had carried him kicking and screaming back to dry land where Nuala waited to enrage him with the toddler version of, 'I told you so.'

'How did you end up working for Sam Morton?' Cristo prompted.

'Pure good luck. I was living at home and working as a personal trainer again. My best client was a friend of Sam's. That kind lady talked me up to him when he was looking for a spa manager and he phoned me and offered me an interview.'

'What made you leave London to return to Oxford?'

Erin shot him a taut glance and opted for honesty. 'I couldn't afford city life when I was living on benefits. I should never have resigned from my job at the Mobila spa—that was rash and short-sighted of me.'

'I was surprised when you resigned,' Cristo admitted. 'Later I assumed it was because you'd been dipping into the till and you thought it would be safer to stage a vanishing act.'

Erin stiffened at that reminder but said nothing, resigned to the fact that she could not combat that charge until she had, at least, tackled Sally Jennings. 'I left because I didn't want to keep running into you and I assumed you'd feel the same way but I was over-sensitive. Leaving after working there such a short time blighted my CV. It was also much harder to find another job than I thought it would be.' Especially once she had realised that she was pregnant and no longer feeling well, she completed inwardly.

A hundred memories of their time together were assailing Cristo and lending a brooding edge to his mood. He remembered her twirling in the rain with an umbrella. She had preferred nights in watching DVDs to nights out at a club but the horror movies, which she

SAVE UP TO 25%

Subscribe to Modern today and get 4 books a month delivered to your door for 3, 6 or 12 months and gain up to 25% OFF! That's a fantastic saving of over £40!

MONTHS	FULL PRICE	YOUR PRICE	SAVING
3	£41.88	£35.61	15%
6	£83.76	£67.02	20%
12	£167.52	£125.64	25%

As a welcome gift we will also send you a FREE L'Occitane gift set worth £10

PLUS, by becoming a member you will also receive these additional benefits:

🌹 FREE Home Delivery

🌹 Receive new titles TWO MONTHS AHEAD of the shops

🌹 Exclusive Special Offers & Monthly Newsletter

🌹 Special Rewards Programme

No Obligation - You can cancel your subscription at any time by writing to us at Mills & Boon Book Club, PO Box 676, Richmond. TW9 1WU.

To subscribe, visit
millsandboon.co.uk/subscriptions

loved, gave her nightmares. He had learned not to mind being used as a security blanket in the middle of the night. They had virtually lived together at weekends when he was in London, his innate untidiness driving her wild while her love of pizza had left him cold. Now he asked himself how well he had ever known her.

The sun beat down on them as they walked around a little hill village, packed with stone houses and narrow twisting alleys. In the cool quiet interior of the tiny ancient church, she lit a candle and said a little prayer for peace while Cristo waited outside for her. Around him she couldn't think straight and the level of her emotional turmoil was starting to scare her. She needed to hate him but what she was feeling was *not* hatred. That she knew, but what she did feel beyond the pull of his magnetic attraction was much harder to pin down and she abandoned the challenge. In twenty-four hours she would be heading home and this little episode would be finished, she reasoned doggedly, keen to ground herself to solid earth again. What was the point in tormenting herself with regrets and foolish questions?

They had a simple lunch in the medieval piazza where Cristo stretched like a lion basking in the midday heat while Erin sat back in the shade, aware that without it her winter pale skin would burn. The waitress, a young woman in her twenties, couldn't take her eyes off the striking beauty of Cristo's classic features or the sizzling effect of his honey-coloured gaze when he smiled. With a sinking heart Erin recalled when she had been even more impressionable.

Even now, she flushed beneath his disturbingly intent scrutiny. '*What*?'

'You look beautiful and you didn't even have to make an effort. It only took you ten minutes to get dressed.'

'You're accustomed to more decorative women... that's all.'

'You always turn aside compliments as though they're insincere,' Cristo murmured, his attention lodging revealingly on the voluptuous curve of her raspberry-tinted lips.

Erin knew that look, recognised his sexual hunger and *felt* the raw pull of it deep inside her body. Her nipples tingled and a pool of liquid heat formed in her pelvis, making her instantly ashamed of her lack of self-discipline. Breathing rapidly in the warm still air in an attempt to suppress those unwelcome reactions, she tensed but she remained insanely aware of his appreciative scrutiny. The atmosphere positively smouldered. Cristo laughed with husky satisfaction and her heart hammered like a trapped bird in her chest.

'Time for us to leave, *koukla mou,*' he murmured, silkily suggestive, sliding fluidly upright to take care of the bill.

Tomorrow could not come soon enough for her, Erin told herself. The weekend would be over and she could pretty much slip back into the comforting routine of her very ordinary life. But she would also be working for Cristo again and in the wake of this forty-eight-hour break from reality that would be no easy challenge.

They walked back downhill, Erin moving a few steps in Cristo's wake. It was the hottest hour of the day and even her light clothing was clinging to her damp skin but she loved the sunshine. He caught her hand as he drew level with the car and drew her closer, hot, hungry eyes with the pure lustre of gold connecting with hers.

He bent his dark head and claimed her lips in a searing kiss. Every response she had fought since leaving the villa bubbled up in a fountain of need. The erotic charge between them was delirious, devastating her defences as he fed hungrily from the sweetness of her mouth. She could feel the leashed demand in his lean, hard body as he bent her back against the car bonnet, the tremor in the long fingers clasping her cheek as her tongue tangled with his. She wanted to eat him alive. With a ragged groan, he stepped back from her.

'Let's go,' he rasped.

Her legs were as bendy and unreliable as twigs as she stumbled into the passenger seat. With her heart thundering and her head swimming after that lusty exchange her thoughts ran blood red with guilt and shame. This was not how she had expected the weekend to turn out: she had never counted on still being so attracted to Cristo that every barrier between them dropped.

Snatching in a steadying breath, Cristo drove off. He felt out of control and he didn't like that. When had 'just sex' become 'must-have sex'? And what had happened to the exorcism goal? *This* was getting her out of his system? He thought of his marriage, an infallible reminder of the danger of undisciplined impulses, and straight away the electrifying heat in his blood cooled, his arousal subsiding to a more bearable level.

Erin's mobile phone started ringing as she entered the villa. She snatched it out of her bag with a frown and answered it. 'Mum?' she queried into the excited barrage of her mother's too fast hail of words. 'Calm down. What is it?'

Cristo watched Erin begin to pace the hall in quick short steps. 'What sort of an accident?' she was asking urgently, her triangular face lint white with shock and dismay. 'Oh m-my…word…how bad is it?'

Erin pressed a concerned hand to her parted lips and turned in a clumsy uncoordinated circle. Nuala had had an accident at the playground and had broken her arm. It was a fracture and required surgery. Erin's heart was beating so fast with worry that she felt sick. Assuring her mother that she would be at the hospital as soon as possible, she ended the call.

'Bad news?' Cristo prompted.

'It's an emergency—you've got to get me home as fast as you can. I'm sorry. I'll go and pack.'

Erin fled upstairs, nothing in her head but the thought of her daughter suffering without her mother's support. She had never felt so guilty in her life. Nuala was hurt and about to have an operation and Erin couldn't be with her. It would never have happened if Erin had stayed at home. Deidre Turner had tried to take the twins to the park in her daughter's place. Nuela had squirmed to the top of the climbing frame and hung upside down in spite of her grandmother's pleas for her to come down. When the child fell she might have broken her arm but she was exceedingly lucky not to have broken her neck. Knowing that her daughter had to be in pain and frightened, Erin felt her tummy churn with nausea. She should have told Cristo that she couldn't make the weekend because she now had children, *responsibilities*. Staying silent on that score had been the act of an irresponsible parent.

'What's going on?' Cristo questioned from the bedroom doorway.

Erin paused in the act of flinging clothes back into her case and twisted her head round. 'How quickly can you get me back home?'

'Within a few hours—we'll leave as soon as you're ready, but I'd appreciate an explanation.'

Erin folded her lips, eyes refusing to meet his, and turned back to her packing. 'I can't give you one. A relative of mine has had an accident and I need to get home…urgently.'

Cristo released an impatient sigh. 'Why do you make such a song and dance about even simple things? Why can't you tell me the whole story?'

Erin dealt him a numb, distanced look. 'I don't have the words or enough time to explain.'

Within fifteen minutes they had left the house to travel to the airport. Erin was rigid with tension and silent, locked in her anxiety about her daughter, not to mention her guilt that her mother was being forced to deal with a very stressful situation alone. This was her punishment for deceiving her mother about where she was staying for the weekend, she thought painfully. Her children needed her but she was not within reach to come quickly to their aid. Instead their next-door neighbour, Tamsin, a young woman with kids of her own, had come to the hospital to collect Lorcan so that her mother could stay on there and wait for Nuala to come out of surgery.

They were walking through the airport when Cristo closed a hand to Erin's wrist and said curtly. 'We have to talk about this.'

'Talking isn't what you brought me here for,' Erin countered tartly. 'I appreciate that you feel short-changed but right now there's nothing I can do about it.'

'That's not what I meant,' Cristo said glacially, frustration brightening his black diamond gaze to brilliance in his lean, strong face. 'I'll get you back to Oxford as quick as I can but you have to tell me what's going on.'

Erin nodded agreement and bit her lip. 'Once we're airborne.'

Tell him—he made it sound so simple. She thought of those phone calls she had made, desperate to tell him, desperate for his support in a hostile world. When she'd realised she was pregnant she had reached out in panic, not thinking about what she would have to say or how he would react. Those kinds of fears would have been luxuries when she was struggling just to survive. Now she was older, wiser, aware she was about to open a can of worms with a blunt knife and make a mess. But why not? Why shouldn't Cristo know that he was a father? How he reacted no longer mattered: she already had a job, a roof over her head. She didn't *need* him any more.

Ensconced in the cream-leather-upholstered luxury of Cristo's private jet, Erin struggled to regain her composure but she was too worried about Nuala and her mother. Deidre Turner didn't deal well with the unexpected and suffered from panic attacks. How could she have left her mother with the burden of the twins for the weekend when the older woman had already looked after them all week long? Her mother would have been tired, tested by the daily challenge of caring for two lively toddlers, who didn't always do as they were told, a combination that was an accident waiting to happen.

Cristo released his seat belt and stood up, six feet four inches of well-groomed male, in a dark business suit that made the most of his lean, powerful physique. Shrewd dark golden eyes below sooty lashes welded to her, he dealt her an expectant look.

'I have children now,' Erin declared baldly, breaking the tense silence. 'Twins of two and a bit, a boy and a girl—'

Unsurprisingly, Cristo was stunned. '*Children*?' he repeated the plural designation in a tone of astonishment. 'How could you possibly have children?'

CHAPTER SEVEN

'THE usual way. I fell pregnant. I became a mother eight months later,' Erin told him flatly.

'Twins?' Cristo bit out a sardonic laugh to punctuate the word.

'Yes, born a little early. And my daughter, Nuala, got hurt in a playground accident this morning. She broke her arm and she has to have surgery on it. That's why I have to get home asap,' Erin completed in the same strained tone.

'And you didn't feel that you could mention the little fact that you're a mother before this point?' Cristo derided grimly.

Erin studied the carpet. 'I didn't think you'd be interested.'

'I'm more interested in finding out who the father of your twins might be,' Cristo admitted, his stubborn jaw line clenching hard. 'Is it Morton?'

'No,' Erin fielded without hesitation. 'My children were very young when I first met Sam.'

'Why is this like pulling teeth?' Cristo demanded with ringing impatience.

'Because you're going out of your way to avoid the most obvious connection.' Erin lifted her chin and stud-

ied him with cool amethyst eyes, an ocean of calm co-
cooning her as she moved towards the final bar she had
set herself to clear. 'Lorcan and Nuala are your children
and don't you dare complain about only finding that out
now! It's your fault that I made endless attempts to get
in touch with you and failed.'

His stunning dark eyes widened, his beautiful mouth
twisting. '*My* children —don't be ridiculous. How could
they possibly be mine?'

'The traditional way, Cristo. You turned over in bed
one night shortly before we broke up and made love
to me without using a condom. Of course I can't be a
hundred per cent certain about the exact timing, but
certainly that's when I assume that I conceived,' she
explained curtly.

Beneath his bronzed skin, Cristo had grown pale as
if such nit-picking detail added a veracity to her claim
that nothing else could have done. 'You're saying that
I got you pregnant?'

'There wasn't anyone else in the picture, in spite of
all your misconceptions about Tom's little brother.' Erin
rose to her feet with determination. 'You are the father
of my children. You can do DNA tests, whatever you
like to satisfy yourself. I really don't care. That side of
things is immaterial to me now.'

Cristo poured himself a drink from the built in bar.
His hand wasn't quite steady as he raised the glass to
his lips and drank deep. 'This is inconceivable.'

He wheeled back round to stare at her with cloaked
intensity, momentarily stepping outside the dialogue
while with every fibre of his being he relived that last
sweet taste of her in sunlight as her tongue tangled with
his. The burn of that hunger had electrified him. She

was a sexual challenge that never waned. That was what she meant to him, a high of satisfaction he craved every time he looked at her. He hated what she was but he wanted to bed her over and over again. That was easier to think about than the fantastic idea that he might have accidentally got her pregnant in the past. Hadn't he only just emerged from a nightmare in that category? A nightmare that had comprehensively blown his marriage and his family apart? And now, the least likely mother of all was telling *him* that he was immaterial? He would never let another woman deny him his paternal rights.

'I'll take a soda and lime,' Erin told him pointedly.

Frowning, his black brows drawing together, Cristo turned back to the bar to prepare her drink. His movements were deft and precise. He handed her a tall moisture-beaded glass, turning his arrogant dark head to study her afresh as he did so. He was so deep in shock at the concept of being a father that he felt as if the passage of time had frozen him in his tracks. 'You said you made endless attempts to get in touch with me.'

'Your PA finally told me that she had instructions not to put my calls through to you and that I was wasting my time.'

Cristo set his glass down on the bar with a sharp little snap of protest. 'I never issued any such instruction!'

'Well, maybe it was the bad fairy who issued it.' Erin lifted and dropped a slight shoulder, unimpressed by his plea of innocence. All too well did she remember how humiliated she had felt having to make those repeated and clearly unwelcome phone calls. 'I also sent a couple of letters.'

'Which I never received.'

Erin ignored that comeback. 'You had changed your

private cell phone number. I had no choice but to try and contact you through your office. At the last, I even phoned your family home in Athens…'

'You contacted my…*parents*?' Cristo queried with frank incredulity.

'And your mother refused to pass on a message to you. She said you were getting married and that you wanted nothing more to do with "a woman like me",' Erin grimaced as she repeated that lowering description.

'I don't believe you. My foster mother is a kind, gentle woman. She would never be so offensive, particularly to a pregnant woman—'

'Oh, I didn't get as far as telling her that I was pregnant during our conversation. I could hardly get a word in edgeways once she realised who I was.'

'She would not have known who you were,' Cristo countered with conviction. 'I never once mentioned your existence to my parents.'

Erin tried not to wince. She had often wondered and he had just confirmed her deepest suspicions. While evidently his foster mother had known her son did have a relationship with a woman in London, she had not received that information from him. Evidently, Erin had never been important enough to her lover to warrant being discussed with his family 'I wrote to your office as well. The letters were returned to me unopened,' she confided doggedly. 'That's when I gave up trying to contact you.'

Cristo drained his glass, set it down, shook his head slightly. 'You say I'm the father of your children. I cannot accept that.'

Erin shrugged and sank back into her seat. At least he wasn't shouting at her or calling her a liar…*yet*. Time might well take care of that oversight. In truth, though, she had never seen him so shaken, for Cristo was strong as steel and given to rolling with the punches that life dealt out. But right now he was in a daze, visibly shattered by her revelation.

'It's OK if you can't accept it. I'll understand. But at least I've finally told you. How you feel about it, whether or not you believe me, isn't relevant any more.'

Cristo shot her an exasperated look that hinted at the darker, deeper emotions he was maintaining control over beneath his forbidding reserve. 'How can it not be relevant?'

'Because it doesn't matter any longer. When I first fell pregnant, life was tough. I needed your help then and I didn't get it,' Erin pointed out ruefully. 'Now, thanks to my mother's support, the kids and I are quite self-sufficient as long as I have a reasonable salary to rely on.'

In the strained silence, Cristo poured himself another drink. She watched the muscles work in his strong brown throat and then recalled how only hours earlier she had wanted to eat him alive and she cringed at that reminder of how weak she could be around him. On the other hand, he was a sophisticated man and he had the sexual experience to make her burn—that was *all*! It would be foolish to punish herself just because she had sunk low enough to enjoy their intimacy on his terms. She was a healthy, warm-blooded woman who had suppressed her natural needs for too long. In the end, if anything, too much self-control had made a victim of her. Of course she had never met a man she wanted as she wanted Cristo, never known a man who, even in the midst of the most emotional scene she had ever endured, could still make her mind wander down undisciplined paths. For there he stood, shocked but unbowed, gorgeous dark eyes smouldering with raw reaction in his even more gorgeous face.

'If this story of yours is true, why didn't you tell me the instant I came back into your life?' he pressed, lifting his proud dark head high, a tiny muscle pulling tight at one corner of his unsmiling mouth.

Erin compressed her lips, shook her head. 'I didn't want anyone to know that we'd even had a past relationship, never mind that you're the father of my kids.'

'I don't follow that reasoning. Would Morton have turned against you had he known the truth?'

'Stop dragging Sam into everything. He's nothing to do with any of this,' Erin said vehemently. 'I owe Sam. He took a risk on me. The job with his hotel group made it possible for me to survive. As for other people knowing about our…er…past connection, I would have found that embarrassing.'

Embarrassing? Cristo gritted his even white teeth while resisting the urge to bite back. Why would she lie now? After all, if he was the father of her twins, he had to owe her thousands of pounds in child support. Nor, until he had made checks, could he disprove her claim that she had tried to contact him to tell him that she was pregnant. If it was true and if she had continued with the pregnancy rather than seeking a way out of her predicament, he owed her a debt, didn't he? While his intelligence urged caution, he would be careful of uttering any disparaging comments.

'I'll accompany you home,' Cristo announced in a tone of finality.

Disconcerted, Erin frowned. 'But why would you do that?'

'Perhaps I would like to see these children whom you insist are my flesh and blood.'

Her triangular face froze, long lashes sweeping down over her eyes while she processed an idea that seemed to strike her as extraordinary.

'Surely you expected that?'

Erin glanced up and clashed with eyes that burned like a furnace in Cristo's hard masculine face. 'I hadn't thought that far ahead.'

'I'm coming to the hospital with you,' Cristo decreed.

Erin winced at the prospect, picturing her mother's astonishment, not to mention the prospect of explaining that she had lied about going to Scotland and had gone to Italy to be with Cristo instead.

'There's nothing else that I can do,' Cristo added grimly.

Erin was mystified. Was curiosity or a sense of duty driving him? But then how on earth had she expected him to react to her revelation? Had she really believed that he might just walk away untouched by the news that he was a father?

'I'm not expecting you to get involved with the twins,' Erin muttered uncomfortably.

'It is more a matter of what I expect of myself,' Cristo countered with a gravity she had never seen in him before.

Oh, my word, what have I done? Erin wondered feverishly. What did he expect from himself in the parenting stakes? His own upbringing, after all, had been unusual. And he was a non-conformist to the marrow of his bones, shrugging off convention if it made no sense to him.

It was nine in the evening before they made it to the hospital. Deidre Turner was seated in a bland little side ward next to a bed in which a small still form lay. The older woman, her face grey with exhaustion and her eyes marked pink by tears, scrambled upright when she saw her daughter. 'Erin, thank goodness! I was scared you mightn't make it back tonight and I was worried about leaving Lorcan with Tamsin,' she confided, only then noting the presence of the tall black-haired male behind Erin.

'Mum?' Erin murmured uncertainly. 'This is Cristo Donakis. He insisted on coming with me.'

For once shorn of his social aplomb, Cristo came to a dead halt at the foot of the bed to gaze down at the little girl with the white-blonde curls clustered round her small head. She looked like Erin but her skin was several shades darker than her mother's fair complexion. His attention rested on the small skinny arm bearing a colourful cast and he swallowed a sudden unfamiliar thickness in his throat. She was tiny as a doll and as he stared in growing wonderment her feathery lashes lifted to reveal eyes as dark a brown as his own.

'Mummy...' Nuala whispered drowsily.

'I'm here.' Erin hastily pulled up a seat and perched on the edge of it, leaning forward to pat Nuala's little hand soothingly. 'How did the surgery go, Mum?'

'Really well. The surgeon was very pleased,' Deidre confided. 'Nuala should regain the full use of her arm.'

'That's a relief,' Erin commented, turning her gaze back to her daughter's small flushed face. 'How are you feeling, pet?'

'My arm's sore.' The little girl sighed, her attention roaming away from her mother to lock to the tall powerful man stationed at the foot of her bed. 'Who is that man?'

'I'm Cristo,' Cristo muttered not quite steadily.

'He's your daddy,' Deidre Turner explained without hesitation, a broad smile of satisfaction chasing the exhaustion from her drawn face.

Shock at that announcement trapped Erin's breath in her throat and she shot the older woman a look of dismay.

'Honesty is the best policy,' Deidre remarked to noone in particular, rising from her seat to extend a hand to Cristo. 'I'm Erin's mother, Deidre.'

'Daddy?' Nuala repeated wide-eyed at the description. 'You're my daddy?'

In the simmering silence, Erin frowned. 'Yes. He's your daddy,' she confirmed. 'Mum? Could I have a word with you in private?'

A nurse came in just then to check on Nuala and, after mentioning that her daughter was complaining of pain, Erin stepped outside with her mother. 'You must be wondering what's going on,' Erin began awkwardly.

'What's there to wonder? Obviously you've finally told the man he's a father and that's not before time,' the older woman replied wryly.

Erin breathed in deep. 'I'm afraid I lied to you about where I was this weekend—I wasn't in Scotland with Tom and Melissa. I was with Cristo.'

'And you didn't know how to tell me, I suppose. Did you think I would interfere?' Deidre enquired astutely. 'He's the twins' father. Naturally you need to sort this situation out but you've taken the first step towards that and I'm proud of you.'

Surprised by that assurance, Erin gave her parent a quick embarrassed hug. 'I'm sorry I wasn't honest with you. Look, now I'm here, you should go home—'

'And collect Lorcan and put him to bed,' Deidre completed. 'He was upset about Nuala. Will you stay the night here with her or will you come home later?'

'I'll see how Nuala is before I decide.'

'She'll be fine. She's a tough little article,' Erin's mother pronounced fondly. 'Lorcan cried when she fell because he got a fright and she called him a baby. By the time I got Nuala to the hospital they were fighting—at least it took her mind off the pain of the break.'

Erin saw the older woman into the lift and returned to the side ward.

'What do daddies do?' Nuala was asking plaintively.

'They look after you.'

Erin's daughter was unimpressed. 'Mummy and Granny look after me.'

'And now you have me as well,' Cristo told his daughter quietly.

'You can fix my arm with magic,' Nuala told him in a tone of complaint.

'Daddy doesn't have his magic wand with him,' Erin chipped in from the foot of the bed.

Nuala's dark eyes rounded. 'Daddy has a magic wand?'

Cristo skimmed Erin a pained glance. 'I'm afraid I don't.'

'Never mind,' Nuala said drowsily. 'My arm hurts.'

'The medicine the nurse gave you will start working soon,' Cristo asserted soothingly.

Within minutes, Nuala had drifted off to sleep.

'I'm sorry Mum just leapt in with her big announcement,' Erin muttered uncomfortably.

'Obviously she believes the twins are mine and, if that's true, there are no regrets on my part,' Cristo responded with a quality of calm she had not expected to see in him after the bombshell she had dropped on him. 'It's a bad idea to lie to children.'

Erin fell asleep in her chair and only wakened when the nurses began their morning round. She was surprised that Cristo had remained through the night, for she had expected him to leave late and make use of a hotel. Instead he had stayed with them and she was grudgingly impressed by his tenacity. His black hair was tousled, his tie loose where he had undone the top button of his shirt. A heavy dark shadow of stubble covered his strong jaw line, accentuating the sensual perfection of his mobile mouth. It shook her to open her eyes and see him and for her first thought to be that he was absolutely gorgeous. Her face flamed as his stunning dark golden eyes assailed hers. Her skin prickled with awareness, her breasts swelling and making her bra feel too tight. She tore her attention from him with a sense of mortification that she had so little control over her reactions to him.

'Apparently the canteen opens soon. We'll go down for breakfast once Nuala has had hers,' Cristo said decisively.

The night had been long and his reflections deep and interminable, Cristo acknowledged heavily, fighting off the exhaustion dogging him. He had watched Erin and the child who might be his daughter sleep. He had remembered the early years of his own childhood with the fortitude of an adult, processing what he had learned from those unhappy memories, already knowing what he must do while striving to greet rather than flinch from the necessity.

Erin took Nuala into the bathroom to freshen up. She was stiff from spending the night in the chair and slow to respond to her daughter's innocent chatter. She did what little she could to tidy herself but her raincoat, silk top and linen trousers were creased beyond redemption and without make-up she could do nothing to brighten her pale face and tired, shadowed eyes.

'Obviously you'll want DNA tests done,' Erin said over breakfast, preferring to take that bull by the horns in preference to Cristo feeling that he had to make that demand. 'I'll agree to that.'

'It would make it easier to establish the twins as my legal heirs,' Cristo agreed, his expression grave. 'But I believe that that is the only reason I would have it done.'

'You're saying that you believe me now?' Erin prompted in a surprised undertone.

Cristo gave her a silent nod of confirmation and finished his coffee. By the time they returned to Nuala's bedside the doctors' round had been done and the ward sister informed them that they could take Nuala home as soon as they liked.

Lorcan, already prepared by his grandmother for the truth that he was about to meet his father, was in full livewire mode, behaving like a jumping bean from the instant Cristo entered the small sitting room of Deidre and Erin's terraced home. Lorcan scrambled onto a stool and stood up to get closer to the tall black-haired male but, dissatisfied with the height differential, leapt off the stool and clambered onto the coffee table instead.

'Get down, Lorcan,' Erin instructed, stooping to gather up the pile of magazines that her son had sent flying to the floor while her mother cooed over Nuala like a homing pigeon. 'Right now...'

When Cristo focused on the little boy he felt as if he had been punched in the stomach. With his coal-black curls and impish dark eyes, Lorcan was a dead ringer for every photograph Cristo had ever seen of himself at the same age. His stare darkened in intensity, shock reverberating through his big powerful length as he made that final step towards accepting what he was seeing as fact: he was a father.

'I'm going to count to five, Lorcan,' Erin warned, her tension level rising. 'One...two...'

Lorcan performed a handstand and grinned with delight at Cristo from upside down. 'Daddy do this?' he asked expectantly.

'*Don't*!' Erin gasped as Cristo bent down.

But, mercifully, Cristo had not been about to perform a handstand. He had merely bent to lift his son off the coffee table and turn him the right side up while Lorcan shrieked with excitement. 'Hello, Lorcan,' Cristo murmured evenly. 'Calm down.'

Unfortunately Lorcan was in no mood to calm down. When Cristo returned him to the floor, Lorcan began to scramble over every piece of furniture in the room at high speed while loudly urging Cristo to watch what he could do. Erin almost groaned out loud as Nuala bounded from her side to try and join in the ruckus. Cristo snatched his daughter out of harm's way. 'Show Lorcan your arm,' he instructed her.

Nuala showed off her cast, small mouth pouting.

'Hurts,' she informed her brother, who moved closer to inspect the injured arm.

Erin crouched down. 'And we have to be *very* careful with Nuala's sore arm,' she told her son.

Lorcan touched the cast enviously. 'Want it,' he said.

'You should take them out to the park to let off some steam,' Deidre Turner suggested, beaming at Cristo, who was returning the cushions Lorcan had knocked off the sofa. 'Oh, never mind about that—I'm used to tidying up every five minutes!'

Erin swallowed a yawn. 'The park? That's a good idea. I'll just go and get changed first.'

Hurtling upstairs to her small bedroom, Erin could not quite come to grips with the knowledge that Cristo was in her home. It felt like some crazy dream but there was something horribly realistic about the fact that both her children were acting up like mad and revealing their every wild and wonderful fault. What did Cristo really think about them? How did he really feel? And why did she care about that side of things? After all, naturally he wanted to see both children to satisfy his curiosity, but she doubted that his interest went much deeper than that. Respecting the cool temperature of a typical English spring, Erin donned straight-leg jeans, knee-length boots and a blue cable knit sweater. She brushed her hair, let it fall round her shoulders and made use of a little blusher and mascara before she felt presentable. Presentable enough for what? *For Cristo*? Shame engulfed her like a blanket. Why was she so predictable? Why was she always worrying about what Cristo thought of her? Only last month she had seen Cristo in a gossip column squiring a beautiful model with hair like gold silk and the glorious shape of a Miss World!

Cristo specialised in superstar women with the kind of looks that stopped traffic. His ex-wife, Lisandra, was an utterly ravishing brunette. Erin had never been in that class and had often wondered if that was why he had lost interest in her.

But now she knew different, she reminded herself wretchedly as she went downstairs. Now she knew that Cristo had dumped her because he believed she was a total slut who had gone behind his back and slept with another man. Was it better to know that or *worse*?

A twin apiece, they walked a hundred yards to the park. Cristo had sent his limo driver off to locate and buy car seats for the children. Lorcan took exaggerated big steps as he concentrated on stepping only on the lines between the flagstones. Nuala hummed a nursery rhyme and pulled handfuls of leaves off the shrubs they passed until Cristo told his daughter to, 'Stop it!'

Without hesitation, Nuala threw herself down on the pavement and began to kick and scream.

'You shouldn't have said that,' Erin hissed in frustration. 'She's tired and cross and her arm's hurting her. Of course she's not in a good mood.'

'You can't let her vandalise people's gardens,' Cristo replied drily and he bent down and picked Nuala up. Her daughter squirmed violently, flailed her fists and screamed full throttle.

Cristo took a couple of fists in the face before he restored order. 'No,' he said again.

'Yes!' Nuala shrieked back at him, unleashing the full tempest of her toddler temper.

Erin was trying not to cringe and cave in to her daughter's every demand as she saw faces appearing at windows overlooking the street.

'Want slide,' Lorcan whinged, tugging at his mother's jacket. 'Want swings.'

'So, this is what it feels like to be a parent,' Cristo commented, flexing his bruised jaw with a slight grimace, his stunning eyes pure black diamond brilliance as if on some weird level he was actually enjoying the challenge.

'They're a handful sometimes…not *all* the time,' Erin stressed, walking on, keen to reach the park where noisy childish outbursts commanded less attention.

Lower lip thrust out, Nuala told Cristo, 'Want down.'

'Say please,' Cristo traded.

'No!' Nuala roared.

'Then I'll carry you the rest of the way like a baby.'

Nuala lost her head again and screamed while her brother chanted delightedly, 'Nuala's a baby!' as he walked by his mother's side.

Silence fell only as they reached the gates of the park.

'Please,' Nuala framed as if every syllable hurt.

Cristo lowered his daughter slowly back onto her own feet.

'I hate you!' Nuala launched at him furiously, snatching her hand free of his and grabbing her mother's free hand in place of it. 'I don't want a daddy!'

As Cristo parted his lips to respond Erin cut in, 'Just ignore it…*please*.'

Once she sat down on the mercifully free bench in her accustomed spot, Erin murmured, 'The best way to handle the twins is with distraction and compromise. Going toe to toe with them simply provokes a tantrum.'

'Thanks for the heads-up. I'm going to need it. I believe I used to throw tantrums,' Cristo confided. 'According to my foster mother, I too was a challenging child.'

'Tell me something I couldn't have guessed.' Erin laughed, abstractedly watching the breeze ruffle his cropped hair into half curls, so very similar to his son's. As she met his spectacular amber and honey coloured eyes framed by sooty lashes, it was as if a hand grabbed her heart and squeezed and possibly that was the moment that she understood that she would never be entirely free of Cristo Donakis. That was not simply because she had given birth to children who had inherited his explosive personality. It was because she enjoyed his forceful character, his strength of purpose and persistence and the very fact he could sit on an old bench in a slightly overgrown and rundown park and seem entirely at home there in spite of his hand-stitched shoes, gold cufflinks and a superbly well-cut suit that still looked a million dollars even after he had sat up all night in it. He might be arrogant but he was hugely adaptable, resourceful and willing to learn from his mistakes.

'I should tell you about my marriage,' Cristo said flatly.

'You never mention your ex-wife,' she remarked helplessly, disconcerted by the sudden change of subject and the intimacy of the topic as she watched Lorcan play on the swings and Nuala head down to the sandpit, her cast protected by the cling film Erin had wrapped round it. It wasn't like Cristo to volunteer to talk about anything particularly private.

'Why would I? We were only married for five minutes and now we're divorced,' Cristo fielded coolly.

'Have you stayed friends?'

'We're not enemies,' Cristo stated after a moment's

thought on that score. 'But we move in different social circles and rarely see each other.'

'Was it a case of marry in haste and repent at leisure?' Erin pressed tautly. 'Did you know her well before you married her?'

'I thought I did.' Cristo bit out a sardonic laugh. 'I also thought it was time I got married. My foster parents, Vasos and Appollonia, had been urging me to marry for a couple of years. It was the only thing they had ever tried to influence in my life and I did want to please them,' he admitted gruffly. 'I met Lisandra at a dinner party at their home. I already knew her but not well. We seemed to be at the same stage in life, bored with the single scene. We got married three months later.'

'So what went wrong?' she almost whispered, recognising the shadow that crossed his lean, darkly handsome face.

'About a year after we married, Lisandra decided that she wanted a child. I agreed—it seemed like the natural next step.' His shapely mouth tightened and compressed. 'When she got pregnant, she was ecstatic and she threw a party to celebrate. Both our families were overjoyed at the prospect of a first grandchild.'

'And you—how did you feel about it?' Erin prompted hesitantly.

'I was pleased, happy Lisandra was happy, grateful she had something new to occupy her. She got bored easily,' Cristo admitted stonily. 'And a couple of months into the pregnancy Lisandra got cold feet.'

'Cold feet?' Erin queried with a frown, her attention locked to the air of harsh restraint etched in his lean strong face that indicated that, while his voice might sound mild, his inner feelings were the exact opposite.

'My wife decided she wasn't ready to have a child after all. She felt too young for the responsibility and trapped by her condition. She decided that the only solution to her regrets and fears was a termination.'

Erin released her pent up breath in a sudden audible hiss. 'Oh, Cristo—'

'I tried to talk her out of it, reminding her that we could afford domestic staff so that she need never feel tied down by our child.' He breathed in slow and deep and bitter regret clouded his dark eyes. 'But I failed to talk her round to my point of view. She had a termination while I was away on business. I was devastated. Our families had to be told. My foster mother, who was never able to have a child of her own, had a nervous breakdown when she found out—she just couldn't handle it. Lisandra's parents were distressed but they supported their daughter's decision because they had never in their entire lives told her that, no, she couldn't have everything and do anything she wanted…'

'And you?' Erin prodded sickly, feeling guilty that she had not even suspected that a truly heartbreaking story might lie behind his divorce.

Cristo linked lean brown hands and shrugged a fatalistic broad shoulder. 'I suppose I couldn't handle it either. Intellectually I don't know what Lisandra and I would have done with a child whose mother didn't want it and resented its very existence but I still couldn't forgive my wife for the abortion. I tried, she tried, we both *tried* but it was just there like an elephant in the room every time we were together. I made her feel guilty, she made me feel angry. I saw too much in her that I didn't like and I didn't think she would ever change, so I asked her for a divorce.'

'I'm so sorry, Cristo…really, very sincerely sorry,' Erin murmured shakily, a lump forming in her throat as she rested a slender hand briefly on his arm in a gesture of support. 'That must have been a shattering experience.'

'I only told you because I want you to understand why I can't walk away from Lorcan and Nuala. If that's what you're expecting or even hoping for, I'm afraid you're going to be disappointed.'

Erin paled, wondering what he was telling her and fearfully insecure about what his next move might be.

CHAPTER EIGHT

CRISTO wasn't accustomed to feeling powerless but that was exactly how he felt after his consultation with a top London lawyer.

An unmarried father, he learned at that crucial meeting, had virtually no rights over his children under English law and even a married father, lacking his wife's support and agreement, might well have to fight through the courts to gain any access to his offspring. Furthermore he had no grounds on which to complain about any aspect of the twins' upbringing. In spite of the fact that he had not contributed to his children's upkeep they were currently living within the security of their mother and grandmother's home with all their needs adequately provided for.

'Marrying the twins' mother is really the only remedy for a man in your position,' he was told succinctly.

It was not good news on Cristo's terms for he loathed any situation outside his control. The DNA testing, achieved and completed within ten days of his first meeting with Lorcan and Nuala had merely confirmed what Cristo already knew and accepted. He was a father and the twins were his flesh and blood, a connection he was incapable of ignoring or treating lightly. He could not move on with his life without them. While he knew that Erin had done her best he also recognised that the twins would require firmer boundaries before they got much older. Yet did that mean that he was to overlook the less acceptable elements in Erin's character? A woman who had stolen from him? For the first time ever he acknowledged grudgingly that that charge did not quite add up. If Erin was mercenary why hadn't she taken more advantage of his financial generosity while she was with him? Why on earth would a woman who craved more money have refused to accept valuable diamond jewellery from him? That made no sense whatsoever. He resolved to take a fresh look at the irregularities that had been found in the accounts of the Mobila spa during Erin's employment there. But before the press got hold of the story—as he was convinced they inevitably would—he required a decent solution, not only to his and Erin's current predicament but also for the future. Some arrangement that would endure for as long as the children needed their parents' support. Recognising the direction his thoughts were taking him in, Cristo felt anger kicking in again.

On the exact same day, Erin was tackling a difficult personal matter with Sam. They were standing in his temporary office, the larger original room having been taken over by a team from Donakis Hotels, who were working to ensure a smooth changeover of ownership. The sale was complete. Sam was only still making himself available for consultation out of loyalty to his hotel group and former employees.

The older man knitted his brows, a shocked look in his blue eyes. 'Cristo Donakis is the twins' father?' he repeated in astonishment.

'I felt I should mention it. My mother has been telling people and I wanted you to hear it from me, rather than as a piece of gossip,' Erin admitted stiffly.

'But when you met here neither of you even admitted that you knew each other.'

'I hadn't seen Cristo since we broke up and my natural inclination was to keep my personal life private.'

Sam Morton dealt her a hurt look that made her flush with discomfiture. 'Even from me?'

'When I walked into your office that day and saw Cristo standing there it was such a shock that I wasn't exactly thinking straight,' she said apologetically. 'I'm sorry. Maybe I should have come clean afterwards but it was very awkward.'

'No, you're quite right. Your private life should be private. I assume it was Cristo you were working for in London?'

Erin nodded. 'I resigned when we split up.'

'I should have made that connection from your original CV. But Donakis let you down badly when you were pregnant,' Sam completed drily.

'There was a misunderstanding,' Erin declared, her eyes evasive. 'Cristo had no idea I was pregnant and there was no further communication between us.'

'But you tried very hard to get in touch with him,' Sam reminded her.

'It was just one of those things, Sam.'

Sam's nostrils flared. 'So, he's forgiven for putting you through hell.'

'It's not like that. Cristo knows about the children now and we're trying to work through that as best we can.'

'Are you getting involved with him again? No, scratch that!' Sam advised abruptly. 'I have no right to pry.'

Erin thought about Italy and screened her expressive eyes. 'I don't know how to answer that question—it's complicated?' she joked uneasily.

'I hope it's the right thing for you. I'd *hate* to see you unhappy again,' Sam pronounced feelingly. 'You gave Donakis one chance. Who's to say he deserves another?'

Well, her mother for one thing, Erin reflected wryly as she caught up with her emails ten minutes later. In her mother's eyes, Cristo had gone from being the most reviled womanising male in Europe to being a positive favourite. And all within the unlikely space of a mere ten days! His regular visits, his interest in the twins, his good manners, his tactful ability to defer to her mother's greater knowledge when it came to the children, his insistence that Deidre Turner join them when they went out to eat had all had an effect. Cristo had shone like a star at every opportunity and was piling up brownie points like a miser with a barn full of treasure chests. Erin, on the other hand, was finding the new order confusing and hard to adapt to.

Cristo was no longer her lover. That weekend in Italy, that single night of passion, did in retrospect seem more like the product of her imagination than anything that had actually happened. Now Cristo visited their home to see Lorcan and Nuala and stayed in one of his newly acquired hotels when he was in the area. He was wary and deep down inside that fact hurt Erin. She could remember another Cristo, a guy who had raced through the door to greet her eagerly when he'd been away for a while, unashamedly passionate, openly demonstrative, not picking his words, not hiding behind caution. This new Cristo was older and much cooler. He was polite, even considerate, but reserved when it came to more personal stuff. Even the confidences he had unexpectedly shared with Erin in the park still troubled her.

His wife's termination had deeply wounded Cristo and possibly made him think more deeply than many men about what a child might mean to him. Now Erin was seeing the results of that more solicitous outlook in practice, for Cristo undoubtedly wanted to do as much as possible to help her with their children. When he visited, he played with them, took them out with Erin in tow and had even helped to bathe them one evening after Erin fell asleep on the sofa after work. He was demonstrating that he could be a hands-on father and the kids were already very partial to his more energetic presence. Erin was impressed but more than a little concerned as to where all this surprising attention was likely to lead.

What did Cristo really want from her? Acceptance of his role? Could it be that simple? Could Cristo, for possibly the very first time in his life, be playing it straight? Or was there a darker, more devious plan somewhere in the back of his mind? Cristo Donakis did not dance to other people's tunes. He always had an agenda. Unfortunately for Erin she was unable to work out what that agenda might be and what it might entail for her and her children. In addition she was especially worried that Cristo still harboured serious doubts about her honesty. It was time she tackled Sally Jennings, she reflected ruefully. Somehow she had to prove her innocence of theft. But would Sally even agree to speak to her? It occurred to her that it might well be wiser to arrive to see Sally at Cristo's flagship London spa without a prior announcement of her intent. She decided to take a day's leave and tackle Sally. Would she get anywhere? She didn't know but it was currently the only idea she could come up with.

The phone by her bed rang at six the following morning and, ruefully knuckling the sleep from her eyes, Erin sat up in bed. '*Yes*?'

It was Cristo. 'Erin?'

'Why are you waking me up at this time of the morning?'

'A deputy editor I'm friendly with has just called me with a tip-off. Apparently there's a story in the pipeline about you, me and the twins. The publication he named is particularly sleazy so I don't think the article will contain anything that your family or mine would want to read.'

Erin's face froze. 'But why? Who on earth would be interested in reading about us?'

'Erin…' Cristo sighed, mustering patience for he was more accustomed to dealing with people who took tabloid attention in their stride and even courted it for the sake of their careers or social status. 'I'm a very wealthy man, recently divorced…'

Lorcan darted through the bedroom door, scrambled under the duvet with his mother and tucked cold feet against her slim thighs. His sister was only a few steps behind him.

Erin was squashed up against the wall as Nuala joined them in the bed. 'If it's true, if there is going to be a story, there's nothing we can do to prevent it.'

'Yes, there is,' Cristo contradicted. 'I can get you and the children out of that house and put you somewhere the paparazzi can't get near you for a photo opportunity. Then I can organise a PR announcement concerning my new status as a father and, once that's done, the press will lose interest.'

Erin breathed in deep. She certainly didn't fancy the press on her doorstep, but she was much inclined to think that he was taking the matter too seriously. 'Cristo, I have a job. I can't just drop everything and disappear.'

'Of course you can. You work for me now,' he reminded her. 'Pack. I'll make the arrangements. A car will pick you up to take you to the airport.'

'But I haven't agreed yet.'

'I will do whatever it takes to protect you and the twins from adverse publicity,' Cristo cut in forcefully, exasperation lending his dark deep drawl a rougher edge. 'I don't want some innuendo-laden piece appearing in print about us.'

'We had an affair. I got pregnant. It's not that unusual—'

'Trust me,' Cristo breathed. 'You'll be accused of having been a married man's mistress and that is not a possibility I want to appear in print.'

A flash of temper and distaste at that prospect rippled through Erin because that was also a humiliating label that she did not want to be lumbered with. 'OK. Where are you planning to send us…assuming I agree, which I haven't yet,' she reminded him.

'Greece…specifically, my island.'

Erin rolled her eyes. 'Oh, so you now have an island all your own?'

'I inherited Thesos from my father when I was twenty-one.'

'Well, you never mentioned it before,' Erin remarked curtly, wondering how much else she didn't know about him while trying to think frantically fast. 'Look, I'll consider going to Greece for a few days if you really think it's necessary—'

'I do.'

'But before I leave I want the chance to speak to Sally Jennings. She does still work for you, doesn't she?'

There was a moment of silence before Cristo responded expressionlessly, 'She does. She's now the deputy manager at the spa. Why?'

'And I'm sure she's very efficient. She was when I was working there,' Erin commented stiffly. 'I'll call in on the way to the airport. I don't want her to know I'm coming. I'll drop the twins off with you at your office.'

'There's no need. I'll meet you in the hotel foyer. But I don't think this is a good idea, Erin. Very few people know about the money that went missing. I handled it very discreetly. I don't think it's wise to start making enquiries again this long after the event.'

'This is the price of me going to Greece,' Erin countered flatly. 'I see Sally in London before I go or I don't go at all.'

'But that's bl—' Cristo retorted in a seething undertone.

'Blackmail?' Erin slotted in with saccharine sweetness. 'You're preaching to the converted, Cristo. Guess who taught me the skill?'

'If I facilitate this meeting at the spa, you'll come to Greece with me?'

'Of course I will. I keep my promises.' Erin came off the phone a minute later, feeling re-energised, and swept the twins out of bed to get dressed. It was past time she began calling some of the shots. Cristo became unbearable when he got his own way too much.

But she was rather touched that he was willing to go to so much trouble to whisk them away from the perils of too much press interest. Honestly, Erin thought ruefully, sometimes Cristo could be naïve. Did he really think she couldn't cope with journalists on the doorstep or some nasty article that tried to make her sound more exciting and wicked than she was? She was not that vulnerable. Life had taught her to roll with the punches. In any case the idea of travelling to Cristo's private island intrigued her. He was *finally* going to take her to his real home and naturally she was curious.

Her mother got up while the twins were eating their breakfast and, when she realised that her daughter was to leave the house in little more than an hour to travel abroad, she urged Erin to go and start packing. Before she did so, Erin rang work and requested a week's leave.

'Do you think you'll meet Cristo's parents?' Deidre asked hopefully.

Erin grimaced, in no hurry to meet Appollonia Denes, who had cut her off on the phone while making it very clear that she did not think Erin was good enough for the little boy she had raised to adulthood. Cristo had been born into a substantial fortune, the only child of two young, rich and beautiful Greeks, both from socially prominent families. Vasos and Appollonia had become Cristo's guardians when he was orphaned at the age of five, after his birth parents died in a speedboat accident. Vasos had been a trusted employee in the Donakis empire and Cristo's godfather. The older couple had had no children of their own. Erin recalled that Cristo had mentioned Appollonia having a nervous breakdown and during that phone call she had decided that the older woman was more than a little off the wall.

So, she hoped she wouldn't be meeting the older couple. Things would be challenging enough without having to deal with people who had disliked and disapproved of her even before they had met her. No doubt Vasos and Appollonia would find the news that she was the mother of Cristo's twins a source of severe embarrassment and dissatisfaction.

The twins fell asleep in the limo that carried them to London, waking up with renewed energy to bounce up the steps of the Mobila hotel. Garbed in a grey pinstripe dress and jacket, her pale hair curving round her cheekbones, Erin was apprehensive as she walked into the opulent foyer.

'Daddy!' Lorcan cried, tearing his hand free of his mother's to pelt across the open space.

'Kisto!' Nuala exclaimed, for she would not call her father Daddy, even though he had asked her to do so.

Erin focused on Cristo, seeing the manager of the renowned hotel anchored to his side and reckoning that so public a greeting from his secret children could scarcely be welcome to him. But Cristo was grinning, that wide wonderful smile she had almost forgotten flashing across his lean bronzed features in a transformation that took her breath away as he swung Lorcan up into his arms and smoothed a comforting hand over Nuala's curly head as she clung to his trouser leg with toddler tenacity.

As Erin looked at the drop-dead gorgeous father of her children a tingle of heat pinched the peaks of her breasts to tightness and arrowed down into her pelvis to spread a sensation of melting warmth. All her hormones, she registered in dismay, were in top working order and threatening to go into overdrive.

'Miss Turner.' The hotel manager shook hands with every appearance of warmth. 'What beautiful children.'

'Erin, I've arranged for Jenny to look after the twins in the crèche while we're visiting the spa,' Cristo explained, and a young woman stepped forward with a smile and proceeded to chat to Nuala.

'So, you've opened a crèche here now,' Erin remarked, her professional interest caught by that idea because she had first floated it to Cristo.

'It's very popular with our clients,' the manger advanced with enthusiasm. 'Many of them have young children.'

'The facility pays for itself,' Cristo explained, a lean hand resting to Erin's taut spine to lead her in the direction of the spa. She was filled with dismay at the realisation that he intended to accompany her, for she had not thought that far ahead and she was convinced that his intimidating presence could only injure her chances of success.

Momentarily. Erin glanced back anxiously at the twins. Lorcan was making a phenomenal noise with the toy trumpet the wily Jenny had produced while Nuala was trying her hardest to get her hands on the same toy.

'Are you certain you want to go ahead with talking to Sally?' Cristo pressed in a discouraging undertone. 'I don't agree with it. What the hell can you expect to gain but embarrassment from such a meeting?'

'Sally is the only person who knows the whole story. I don't have a choice,' Erin replied tightly, her nervous tension rising as Cristo bent down to her level and the rich evocative smell of his cologne and him ensnared her on every level.

'Don't do this for me, *koukla mou*,' Cristo urged suddenly, staring down at her as they came to a halt outside the door that now bore Sally's nameplate. 'It doesn't matter to me now. A lot of water has gone under the bridge since then. You were young. You made a mistake and I'm sure you learned from it—'

'Don't you dare patronise me, you…you…you *toad*!' Erin finally selected in her spirited retort. 'And don't interfere.'

'Toad?' Cristo repeated blankly.

'I'd have called you something a good deal more blunt if I hadn't trained myself not to use bad words around the children!' she told him curtly, hastily depressing the door handle of the office before she could lose what little remained of her momentum.

Sally, a tall middle-aged woman with red hair and light blue eyes, was standing behind her desk talking on the phone. When she saw Erin, she froze, her previous animated expression ironed flat as she visibly lost colour.

'Erin, my goodness,' she breathed in astonishment, dropping the phone back on its cradle in haste and bustling round the desk. 'And Mr Donakis…'

'I would like your assurance that anything that is said in this room remains between these four walls,' Cristo said quietly.

Sally looked bewildered and then she smiled. 'Of course, Mr Donakis. Take a seat and tell me what I can help you with.'

Erin was so nervous that she could feel her knees trembling and she linked her hands tightly together as she sat down. 'I'm sure that you're aware that the audit two and a half years ago threw up certain anomalies in the spa accounts…'

If possible, Sally went paler than ever and she dropped rather heavily back down behind her desk. 'Mr Donakis did ask me to keep that problem confidential.'

'Sally,' Erin muttered, suddenly filled with a sense of utter hopelessness. What craziness had brought her here to this pointless encounter? There was no way Sally was going to offer up a belated confession of fraud with her employer present. 'Perhaps you could leave us alone, Cristo.'

'No, I have news to share first. I'm planning to have the account irregularities looked at again.'

The older woman's face went all tight. 'But, Mr Donakis, I thought that matter was done and dusted. You said you were satisfied.'

'I'm afraid I wasn't. And bearing in mind how helpful you were during the first investigation, I thought you should be informed before the experts arrive to go over the books again,' Cristo completed.

Sally had turned an unhealthy colour, her dazed eyes flickering between the two of them, and suddenly she spoke. 'You're a couple again, aren't you?' she exclaimed, her attention lodging almost accusingly on Erin. 'And you've told him about me, haven't you?'

'Told me what?' Cristo enquired lazily.

Taking on board the reality that Cristo was piling the pressure on Sally to admit that she had lied and offering Erin a level of support she had not expected to receive from him, Erin squared her shoulders in frustration. She had always fought her own battles.

Sally compressed her lips in mutinous silence as if daring Erin to answer that question.

'While I was working here I discovered that Sally had been taking products from the store and selling them on online auctions.' Erin turned her attention back to the older woman, who had once been a trusted colleague. 'I know I promised that that was our secret but sometimes promises have to be broken.'

'You were stealing?' Cristo prompted Sally forbiddingly.

Tears spilled from Sally's eyes and she knocked them away with her hand and fumbled for a tissue, which she clenched tightly in one hand.

'I guarantee that whatever you tell me there will be no prosecution now or in the future.' Lean, strong face taut, Cristo stood up, a lithe powerful figure of considerable command. 'I very much regret that you felt unable to be honest with me when this business was first discovered but I'm hoping that for Erin's sake you will now tell me the truth.'

'No prosecution?' Sally queried uncertainly.

'No prosecution. I only want the truth,' Cristo confirmed.

'One lunchtime shortly before Erin resigned a man came to see me,' Sally related in a flat voice. 'He said he was a private detective and he offered me a substantial amount of money if I could give him information that would damage Erin's reputation.'

'*What*?' Cristo positively erupted into speech, his disbelief unhidden.

'His name was Will Grimes. He worked at an agency in Camden. That's all I know about him. At first I said no to him. After all there wasn't any information to give!' Sally pointed out with a wry grimace. 'You hadn't done anything but work hard here, Erin, but then you suddenly resigned from your job and just like that I realised how I could get myself out of the trouble that I was in.'

'Will Grimes,' Cristo was repeating heavily.

'I was in a great deal more financial trouble than I admitted when you found me helping myself to that stuff from the store,' Sally told Erin tautly. 'I had set up a couple of other scams in the books—'

'The payments to therapists that didn't exist, the altered invoices?' Cristo specified.

'Yes, and then you organised the audit and I started to panic,' Sally confided tearfully. 'Erin had left the spa by then.'

'And you decided to let me take the blame for it?' Erin prompted while she wondered how on earth she had ever attracted the attention of a private detective.

'I *wanted* to stop taking the money,' the older woman stressed in open desperation.' I knew it was wrong but I had got in too deep. Once the fraud was uncovered and I set up things so that you got the blame I could go back to a normal life again and, of course, I still had my job. I knew you would be safe from prosecution with Mr Donakis—he wasn't likely to trail his own girlfriend into court!'

'You got me right on that score,' Cristo derided.

'Will you prosecute me now?' Sally asked him shakily.

'No. I gave you my word and I thank you for finally telling me what really happened,' Cristo responded.

Clearly limp with relief, Sally braced her hands on the desk to stand up. 'I'll clear my desk immediately and leave—'

'No, work out your notice here as normal,' Cristo

urged, resting a hand on Erin's taut shoulder to ease her slowly upright.

'Erin?' Sally breathed stiltedly. 'I'm sorry. When you were so kind to me, you deserved better from me.'

Erin nodded, even tried to force her lips into a forgiving smile, but couldn't manage it for she was all too well aware how the false belief that she was a thief had affected Cristo's opinion of her. In any case, she was deeply shaken by what Sally had confessed and she couldn't hide the fact. She had been fond of the older woman, had only lost contact with her because she had fallen pregnant and on hard times. Pride had ensured that she did not pursue ongoing contact with anyone at her former workplace. She stole a veiled glance at Cristo's profile. He was pale, his facial muscles taut below his dark complexion.

Cristo paused at the door on his way out. 'Did you collect the reward money from the private detective and give him the supposed evidence of Erin's dishonesty?'

Sally winced and nodded slowly. 'It got me out of debt and gave me a fresh start.'

Erin gritted her teeth, disgusted by Sally's selfishness.

Cristo felt as if the walls of his tough shell were crumbling around him. Astonishingly, Erin's seemingly paranoid suspicion that she was being set up for a fall by persons unknown had been proven correct. He, who rarely got anything wrong, had been wrong. He had made an appalling error of judgement. But more than anything at that moment he wanted to know who could possibly have hired a detective to discredit Erin in his eyes by fair means or foul.

CHAPTER NINE

Erin picked at the perfectly cooked lunch served on board Cristo's private jet without much appetite. She was still angry at Sally and bitter that the older woman had got away with destroying Erin's reputation rather than her own. How many other people were suffering from the mistaken assumption that she was a con woman, who had escaped her just deserts solely because she was the owner's ex-girlfriend? As someone who had always worked hard with scrupulous honesty and pride in her performance of her duties, she deeply resented the false impression that Sally had created to hide her own wrongdoing.

'We have to talk,' Cristo remarked flatly.

'I don't think I've ever heard that phrase from you before,' she parried waspishly, recalling that once upon a time Cristo had been the first out of he door when such a suggestion was laid before him. That had certainly been his all-too-masculine reaction on every occasion when she'd tried to corner him for a *serious* conversation.

From the cabin next door she could hear the sounds of the children playing and talking. Jenny, the charming young brunette nanny, had turned out not to work for the spa crèche after all. No, indeed, Jenny had been specifically hired by Cristo to take care of the twins while they were in Greece.

'That's so unnecessary and extravagant,' Erin had criticised when she found out about the arrangement at the airport.

'You can't look after them 24-7,' Cristo had informed her authoritatively.

'Why can't I?' she had asked.

'Why shouldn't you have a break?' he had responded arrogantly.

'If Jenny is your concept of responsible parenting you need to buy another handbook,' she had retorted curtly, annoyed that he had taken such a decision over her head. He was Lorcan and Nuala's father: all right, she accepted that, however that didn't mean that she would accept his interference in matters about which he was scarcely qualified to have an opinion. She was no more in need of a break than any other working mother, she thought thinly, which she supposed meant that, rail as she had at him, the prospect of the occasional hour in which she could relax and think of herself again was disturbingly appealing and made her feel quite appallingly guilty.

Returning to the present and the tense atmosphere currently stretching between them, Erin shot Cristo a glance from cool amethyst eyes. 'You think we should talk? I'll be frank—only if you crawled naked over broken glass would I think you had redeemed yourself.'

A wicked grin very briefly slashed Cristo's lean bronzed features, his dark eyes shot with golden amusement below his thick sooty lashes, making him spectacularly handsome. 'Not much chance of that,' he admitted.

'So, where's my apology?' Erin demanded truculently to mask the effect of her dry mouth and quickened heartbeat because, no matter how furious he made her, she could still not remain impervious to his stunning good looks, a reality that mortified her. 'It's taking you long enough!'

'I was trying to come up with the right words.'

'Even if you swallowed a dictionary, it wouldn't help you!'

Lean strong face taut, Cristo sprang out of his seat. 'I am sincerely sorry that I ever entertained the suspicion that you had stolen from me, *koukla mou*.'

'You didn't just entertain it,' she objected. 'You fell for it hook, line and sinker!'

'My security team are even at this moment checking into this Will Grimes angle. I can't understand why a private detective would have been interested in you.' Indeed, having thought deeply about that particular issue, Cristo could only think that someone *he* knew had hired a detective in an apparent effort to disgrace Erin. But who would have wasted their money on such a pursuit and what had been the motivation? It still made no sense to him. Erin had not been his wife or fiancée? Why would anyone have wanted to harm her and, through her, him?

Erin tilted her chin, eyes glinting pure lavender. 'Seems I wasn't paranoid, after all. I'm still waiting on that apology too.'

His strong jaw line hardened, dark eyes gleaming. 'And you'll be waiting a long time because you're not getting a second. If you hadn't been so direct about your expectations I might have soft-pedalled for the sake of peace, but now I'll be equally direct: you brought that theft accusation down on your own head!'

Erin stared at him aghast, totally wrong-footed by that condemnation coming at her out of the blue when she had expected a grovelling apology. *Really*? Well, possibly not of the grovelling variety, but, yes, she had assumed he would be embarrassed by his misjudgement and eager to soothe her wounded feelings. Now, deprived of that development and outraged by his attitude, Erin leapt out of her seat to face him. 'And how do you work that out?'

'As far as I was aware Sally Jennings was an exemplary long-term employee with no strikes against her and no reason to lie. Had I known she had already been caught thieving at work I would have known to take a closer look at her activities,' Cristo shot back at her levelly.

Erin stiffened, feeling she was on weaker ground when it came to the decision she had once made over Sally and defying the reflection. 'Sally was going through a divorce and she has two autistic sons. At the time, I believed she needed compassionate handling rather than punishment.'

Cristo expelled his breath in a hiss, his brilliant eyes cracking like whips. 'Compassion? If I'd known then how you mishandled her dishonesty I would have sacked you for incompetence!'

'*Incompetence*?' Erin bleated incredulously, rage jumping up and down inside her like a gushing fountain suddenly switched on.

'Yes, incompetence,' Cristo confirmed with succinct bite. 'How would you feel about a manager who left a thief in a position of power in your business and chose not to warn anyone about her dangerous little weakness?'

'I dealt with the situation as I saw fit back then. Looking back, I can see I was too trusting—'

'Correction…bloody naïve!' Cristo shot back at her witheringly. 'I didn't hire you to be compassionate. Plenty of people lead tough lives but few of them steal. I hired you to take care of part of my business and that was your sole responsibility. Listening to sob stories and letting a clever calculating woman get off scot-free with her crimes was no part of your job description!'

It took enormous will power but Erin managed to restrain her temper and the urge to snap back at him because she knew that he was making valid points. 'It's not a decision I would make now. Unfortunately I liked Sally and believed she was a wonderful worker. I was naïve—I'll admit that—'

'Why the hell didn't you consult me about it or at least approach someone with more experience for their opinion on what to do about her?' Cristo demanded angrily. 'At the very least, once you knew Sally was a thief, all her activities at work should have been checked out thoroughly and she should have been moved to a position where she had no access to products, account books or money.'

As he made those cogent decrees Erin lifted her head high, refusing to go into retreat. 'You're right but I thought I could deal with the situation on my own. I didn't want you to think that I couldn't cope. But I was hugely overworked and stressed at the time. I notice the current manager has a deputy and I saw at least two administrators in the general office. I didn't have anyone but Sally to rely on.'

'Then you should have asked for more help,' Cristo fielded without hesitation.

'My biggest mistake was accepting a position from someone I was involved with. I was too proud, too busy trying to impress you about what a great job I was doing. I didn't have enough experienced staff around me and those that were there kept their distance because I was too close to the boss. I was very focused on building the business, bringing in more custom, increasing productivity. It made me far too dependent on Sally for support. I can see that now,' Erin concluded that honest statement curtly.

'At least you can now see what that inappropriate decision cost you. Sally didn't hesitate when it came to setting you up to take the blame for her acts of fraud or when she got the chance to reap financial benefits from her disloyalty,' Cristo pointed out.

'Don't forget that Sally Jennings fooled you as well. The role she played was very convincing,' Erin reminded him tightly. 'You didn't smell a rat in her performance either.'

'But I would have done had you tipped me off about her stealing. Right, we've aired this for long enough, subject closed,' Cristo pronounced decisively.

'Now that you've had your say and blamed me for everything?' Erin countered tautly, amethyst eyes dark and unwittingly vulnerable, for that word, 'incompetence', had cut deep as a knife. 'Was it too much for me to expect that after knowing me for a year you would question the idea that I might have been filling my pockets at your expense?'

'After certain suspicions had been awakened and the man I saw in your hotel-room bed I will concede that I was predisposed to think the worst of you,' Cristo derided, compressing his wide sensual mouth into a tough line. 'What's that cliché about the easiest explanation usually being the right one? In this case, the easiest explanation was the wrong one.'

Erin sank back down in her seat. 'Am I finally getting a clean slate on the score of the one-night stand with the toy boy?' she asked grittily. 'Tom's brother, Dennis, was only nineteen back then.'

'That's not quite so clear cut. My suspicions in that quarter were first awakened by other indications, which I will discuss with you when we get to the island,' he added as her triangular face tensed into a frown of bemusement. 'I am sincerely sorry that I misjudged you and that I didn't dig a little deeper three years back.'

Erin said nothing. What other evidence of her infidelity did he imagine he had? She hadn't a clue what he was talking about and had no time for more mysteries. In addition her mind was being bombarded with thoughts after that heated exchange of views. He had shot her down in flames and it rankled and that was precisely why she had not approached him for advice after she had caught Sally stealing. She had known he would take the toughest stance and would call in the police. She had feared that he would blame her for the inadequate security in the products store, which had made Sally's thefts all too easy. If she was honest she had also worried about how she would cope without Sally at her elbow. My mistake, she acknowledged painfully. A wrong decision that had cost her more than she could ever have dreamt.

Cristo watched in frustration as Erin made a weak excuse and went off to join Jenny and the twins. It had been right to tell her the truth, he told himself angrily. He was damned if the fact that she was the mother of his children would make him start lying just to please her! Did shooting from the hip mean he had also shot himself in the foot? Almost three years ago, he had not talked to Erin about important issues and this time around he was determined not to repeat that mistake. Blunt speech had to be better than minimal communication and misunderstandings, he decided impatiently.

Shielded by the need to keep the twins occupied for what remained of a journey that entailed a final helicopter flight to the island of Thesos, Erin licked her wounds in private. From the air she had a fantastic view of Cristo's island. It was bigger than she had imagined and the southern end was heavily forested with pine trees. She spied a cluster of low-rise structures on what appeared to be a building site on the furthest coast and a picturesque little town by the harbour before the helicopter flew level again and began to swoop down over the tree tops to land.

Lorcan was asleep and Cristo hoisted his son out of Erin's arms and carried him off. They had landed about twenty yards from a magnificent ultra-modern villa surrounded by terraces and balconies to take advantage of the land and sea views.

'This all looks new,' Erin remarked.

'I demolished my parents' house and had this one designed about three years ago. It made more sense than trying to renovate the old place,' he commented casually.

Three years ago, while they had still been a couple, Erin had known nothing about his island or the new house he was having built. Not for the first time Erin appreciated that Cristo had shut her out of a large section of his life and she wondered why. Obviously he had never considered her important enough to include her in the Greek half of his existence, which encompassed home and family. And that, whether she liked it or not, *hurt*, most particularly when he had married a Greek woman within months of dumping Erin.

A short brunette with warm brown eyes was introduced as Androula, the housekeeper. Straight away Androula cooed over the children in their arms and hurried off to show Erin and Jenny to the rooms set aside for their use. Erin was taken aback to discover that Cristo had already had accommodation specially prepared for his son and daughter, each complete with small beds, appropriate decoration and an array of toys. Leaving the capable Jenny to put the drowsy children to bed, Erin explored her own room with its doors opening onto the terrace and superb view through the trees to a white beach and a turquoise sea over which the sun was sinking in a display of fiery splendour.

'Will you be comfortable here?'

Erin spun to find Cristo behind her, poised between the French windows. 'How could I fail to be? It's the height of luxury,' she said awkwardly.

Cristo searched her shuttered face and breathed almost roughly, 'I was tough on you on the plane. I was angry that you let that scheming woman make you pay the price for her crimes.'

'But at least that's sorted out now. The rooms organised for the children are beautiful,' she told him stiffly, suppressing the discomfiture she was still feeling. 'You must have organised that almost as soon as you found out about them.'

Cristo inclined his dark head. 'Yes, even before I asked you if they could visit Thesos. I still tend to act first and ask later.'

Not even questioning that arrogant assumption of power, Erin turned away and rested her elbows back on the low wall girding the terrace. She had intended to get her revenge on Cristo for what he had done to her in Italy, but it had gradually dawned on her that angering or hurting Cristo would most probably damage his relationship with their children. Their own relationship was irrevocably meshed with the ties and responsibilities of also being parents. And how, in conscience, could she take that risk of weakening those links?

'You never ever told me that this place existed,' she said.

'What would have been the point if I wasn't planning to bring you here?' he murmured wryly. 'When I was with you I wasn't quite ready to move our affair on to the next stage. I was simply enjoying the place we had reached until it blew up in both our faces. I'm sorry.'

'No need to apologise.' Erin fought the just-slapped-in-the-face sensation of humiliation that his piece of plain speaking inspired and wondered why on earth he was suddenly telling her such things. In the past she had loved him and longed for a secure future with him but he had not felt the same. Why did that news still make her feel so gutted? That time was gone and she didn't love him any longer. She just lusted after him, enjoyed his energising company, respected his business prowess, intelligence and strength of principle. Enumerating that unacceptably long list of his supposed attributes, Erin gritted her teeth together. Why was she doing this to herself? Dwelling on things that no longer had any place between them? She was the mother of his children and that was all.

'In those days…' Cristo, engaged in watching the tense muscles in her slender back and the vulnerable piece of pale nape exposed by her bent head, floundered. 'I wasn't exactly in touch with my feelings.'

'I'm not sure you had any…above your belt,' Erin specified shakily.

'That is *so* wrong!' Cristo growled, lean hands closing forcefully to her shoulders to tug her back round to face him. 'I was sick to the stomach when I thought you'd gone to bed with another man! It turned my whole life upside down!'

'Try being pregnant by a man you can't even get to speak to you on the phone!' Erin lanced back at him with unconcealed bitterness.

His dark golden eyes shone amber bright at the challenge. 'I would never have knowingly allowed that to happen. What reason would I have to treat you like some demented stalker? I intend to get the full story out of Amelia when I'm next in Athens where she works now.'

'I'll still never forgive you.'

His superb bone structure was taut and he gazed steadily back at her. 'Was being pregnant so bad?'

'I had to live on welfare benefits. It was a struggle I'll never forget,' Erin admitted truthfully. 'My home was a damp tenth-floor council flat barely fit for human habitation. It was only when my mother came to see me and realised how I was living that she invited me to go home with her. There was also the not so little matter of me being pregnant and unmarried, which really did upset Mum. She's an old-fashioned woman and as far as she's concerned decent girls don't have babies until they have a ring on their wedding finger. We were estranged for most of my pregnancy.'

His concern was unfeigned. 'You had no support at all? What about your friend, Elaine? Did she ask you to move out of her apartment?'

'No, I made that decision— I couldn't pay my way any more,' Erin explained ruefully. 'But Tom and Melissa helped out as best they could.'

'Melissa?'

'Now Tom's wife but at the time they were living together and I couldn't have had better friends,' Erin declared. 'They were very good to me.'

His keen gaze was screened by his luxuriant black lashes, his eloquent mouth set in a forbidding line. 'I owe them a debt for that.'

'Yes, you do,' Erin told him bluntly. 'They didn't have much either but what they had they shared.'

His lashes swept up on breathtakingly beautiful golden eyes from which all anger had vanished. 'But I owe the biggest debt of all to you for bringing my children into the world. Don't think I don't appreciate that and know how lucky I was that you chose not to have a termination. I *do* know—I *do* appreciate it,' he completed in a rare display of unmistakable emotion.

Cristo took the wind out of Erin's sails with that candid little speech, but her anger with him was not so easily soothed. 'When I was pregnant I assumed that if you had a choice you would have preferred me to have a termination. You once told me about that friend of yours whose girlfriend got pregnant,' she reminded him.

'I didn't say that I approved of what they chose to do. Maybe it was right for them but I would not have reacted the same way that he did.'

'Easy to say,' she needled. 'Hindsight is a wonderful device with which to rewrite the past. You also said that you preferred your life without baggage.'

'Don't judge me for what I did and didn't do almost three years ago. I've grown up a lot since then,' Cristo spelt out tautly.

His marriage to Lisandra, she thought ruefully, thinking it was sad that she apparently owed this rather less arrogant and reserved version of Cristo to the machinations of another woman. Even so, her heart could only be touched by his gratitude that she had given birth to Lorcan and Nuala. She had felt his sincerity and it meant a great deal to her. Cristo had, after all, taken to fatherhood with enthusiasm and energy. He seemed neither resentful of the responsibility he had had thrust on him, nor ill-at-ease with it. That awareness tore more than one brick out of Erin's defensive wall.

Walking back indoors, she noticed a trio of large envelopes lying on an occasional table. Already opened, they were addressed to Cristo at his London office. 'What are these?'

Cristo hesitated and then frowned, his restive pacing coming to a sudden halt. 'The evidence I promised to show you once we got here. Take a look at what's in those envelopes…'

'Why? What's in them?'

'Photos which were sent to me during the latter months we were together in London.'

Erin extracted a large, slightly blurred photograph of a couple walking hand in hand. The man was her friend, Tom Harcourt, and the face on the woman was hers. As she had never held hands with Tom in her life she was astonished until she studied the body and the clothing of the female depicted. In a frantic rush, she leafed through the other photos, one showing the same couple kissing and another of them hugging. 'That may be my face but it's not my body—it's Melissa's. These photos are all of Tom with his wife, Melissa, but they've been digitally altered to make it look as though the woman is me!' she murmured in disbelief.

'*Altered*?' Cristo stood by her side as she fanned out the photos and one by one proceeded to verbally pick them apart. 'How altered?'

'Whoever sent these photos to you grafted my face onto Melissa's body,' she told him angrily. 'All we have in common is that we're both blondes but I'd recognise that sweater from a mile away! How on earth could you think that was me, Cristo? Melissa is much smaller, well under five foot tall. Didn't you notice how small she seems beside Tom, who isn't that tall? And since when did I have a bust as big as that?'

Peering down at the photos, Cristo noted every point of comparison. 'None of them are of you with Tom,' he finally breathed in bewilderment. 'Why didn't I notice those differences for myself?'

It might as well have been a rhetorical question because Erin had no intention of pursuing that pointless line of enquiry. 'As you said, you act first and ask later. But I just don't believe how secretive you can be! You received these rotten lying photos on three separate occasions and didn't once mention them to me. No wonder you became so suspicious of my friendship with Tom!'

In retrospect she could recall the surprisingly sudden alteration in Cristo's attitude towards her spending time with Tom while he was away on business. Cristo had gone from accepting that friendship without comment to suddenly questioning her every meeting with the other man, but only now was she discovering that genuine disquiet had provoked that change of heart.

Erin was struggling to understand why he had remained silent in the face of such provocation and failing. It was cruel to realise that she had gone through so much pain just because some hateful individual had decided to destroy Cristo's trust in her, ensuring that he would reject her. He had walked away from her and almost straight away gone on to marry another woman. The wound inflicted by that decision of his had never left her. He had got over her so quickly and she believed that he must always have viewed her as not being good enough to marry. His choice of a rich Greek wife from a background similar to his own had been revealing.

'Why didn't you show these photos to me at the time?' Erin demanded.

Lean, strong face shuttered, Cristo clenched his jaw. He walked away a few paces, his long, lean body as fluid and graceful as running water, his black hair gleaming like polished jet in the fading daylight above his bold bronzed profile. Sometimes he looked so incredibly handsome that she couldn't take her eyes off him, she thought rawly, anguish for what they had lost engulfing her.

'I had too much pride,' Cristo grated the admission. 'I could not make my mind up about whether you were cheating on me or whether your relationship with Tom had simply become too close and affectionate. I didn't know what to think but it did make me doubt your loyalty—'

'And when you walked into that hotel room and saw a strange man in the bed, you were in exactly the right frame of mind to assume that I was cheating on you,' Erin completed with fierce resentment. 'How could you not give me a single chance to defend myself?'

'I will always regret it,' Cristo confessed in a driven undertone, piling the photos together and cramming them into a single envelope. 'We are now living with the consequences. I've missed more than two years of my children's lives as a result. I would not like to be in the shoes of whomever I find is responsible for deliberately setting out to destroy us.'

'But the hotel-room thing was just an unlucky co-incidence,' Erin reasoned heavily, shaken that anyone could have gone to such lengths to discredit her in his eyes. 'I do understand after seeing those photos that you honestly believed you didn't need to see me in the flesh in the same room to believe that I was cheating on you. Do you have a bunny-boiling ex-girlfriend somewhere in your past? Jealous women can be vicious. Who else would take so much time and trouble and put so much money into trying to split us up?'

'I don't know but I have every intention of finding out,' he swore, a hostile expression stamped on his hard features. He cast the envelopes aside and drew her back to him with determined hands.

He lowered his head and caressed her parted lips slowly with his own in a move that completely disconcerted her. Her entire body tingled with electrified awareness. Coming alive to his sensual call, she was shamefully aware that the peaks of her breasts were straining into bullet points and her thighs pressing together to contain the ache of emptiness there. 'I want a fresh start with you,' he breathed in a raw undertone, his breath fanning her cheek. 'Let's get all the rubbish out of the way and leave it behind us.'

'A lot of what you call rubbish messed up my life,' Erin replied defensively, her eyes prickling with tears behind her eyelids, and she didn't even understand why she so suddenly felt screamingly vulnerable and unsure of herself. *I want a fresh start with you.* She hadn't seen that coming, didn't know what to say.

'We both screwed up,' Cristo contradicted, gravity hardening his high cheekbones to make him look tougher and stronger than ever. 'We can't change the past but we can begin again…'

Erin looked up into his lean, tense features. 'Can we?' she whispered.

Long brown fingers framed her cheekbone and intent dark golden eyes flamed over her troubled face. 'I say we can,' he declared, curving a hand to her hip to ease her closer.

She wanted to believe it; she wanted to believe it so badly. He wanted her back. He *still* wanted her. A powerful tide of relief rolled through her, closely followed by a flood of happiness. Dark eyes glinting sensually below his lashes, he melded her to his big powerful length and desire flared through her like a hungry fire ready to blaze out of control. The heat of him against her, the glorious scent of his skin and the hungry thrust of his erection were a potent inducement and when he crushed her sultry mouth beneath his she was with him every step of the way.

Cristo peeled off her blouse with wildly impatient hands and then released her bra to bury his mouth urgently in the sweet sloping swell of her breasts. 'You're so beautiful, so perfect—'

'Not perfect,' she protested as he gathered her up and lowered her down on the bed with a scantily leashed impatience she could not resist.

'You're perfect for me, *koukla mou*,' Cristo countered, determined to have the last word. 'You always were.'

The passionate kiss that followed as he explored the confines of her mouth with devouring heat silenced her. Her nipples were hard and swollen and he dallied there with his mouth and his fingers to reduce her to gasping compliance with the hot sensuality that was so much a part of him. The remainder of her clothes were discarded and Cristo undressed in haste, returning to claim her with his lean, strong body boldly aroused. Her heart raced as she stroked the long, hard thickness of his shaft and she rejoiced when he groaned and arched his hips up to her in supplication. He flipped her back against the pillows, searching out the slick sensitive folds and the tiny knot of nerve-endings above to stroke her with teasing, tender skill. The tide of pleasure swept her out of her control, each touch of his fingers making her burn and writhe and finally sob with anticipation and need. And only then did he reach for protection and sink deep into her damp sheath, telling her huskily of his pleasure as her inner muscles tightened convulsively around him. Excitement gripped her when he withdrew and then plunged deep into her again, ripples of delight rising higher and higher inside her as the fire in her pelvis burned hotter than ever. And when she finally reached a climax and he reached the same point with her, he lay sated and uncharacteristically silent in the protective circle of her arms afterwards and she felt gloriously happy.

'That was…wonderful, *koukla mou*,' Cristo husked, folding her slight damp body, to him with possessive arms. 'I don't know how I contrived to keep my hands off you for so long.'

'I should've said no,' Erin lamented, studying his lean, darkly handsome features with dazed eyes. 'You blackmailed me into bed in Italy—'

'You wanted me.' Cristo punctuated that claim with a soothing kiss on her reddened lips, smouldering golden eyes scanning her flushed face with unashamed satisfaction. 'I wanted you. I found a way round the difficulties so that we could be together again. Now that I have you back in my arms where you belong I would be a liar if I pretended to have regrets.'

'The end justifies the means?' Erin pressed drily.

'You know that you want me just as much,' he argued with unashamed assurance. 'When we burn, we burn together.'

It was true and even with that frantic need fulfilled she could not lie in contact with that compellingly masculine body of his without experiencing the first little quivers of yet another sensual awakening. As the liquid warmth at the heart of her began to melt he ran the edge of his teeth down the extended length of her neck and she shivered violently. He reached for another condom and then pulled her over to him, watching as her lashes dipped low in a cloaked expression of intense pleasure that he savoured.

'Will you marry me?' he murmured tautly.

Eyes flying wide, Erin stared down at him, wondering if she had imagined that question.

'It seemed like the right moment,' Cristo asserted, his hands clasping to her hips to rock her gently up on him and then down in a controlling rhythm that was impossibly exciting. 'Don't laugh—'

'I'm not going to laugh!' she riposted, offended by the suggestion and studying him with troubled amethyst eyes. 'Are you serious?'

'I want you and the twins to be a proper part of my life.' His breathing fractured as she made a subtle circling movement above him, pale silvery fair hair streaming down over her shoulders to allow tantalising glimpses of her small pert breasts. 'I don't think it can get better than this, *koukla mou*.'

And when only minutes later yet another orgasm took Erin by storm, she decided she agreed with him. She lay in the relaxed circle of his arms, breathing in the hot damp smell of him like a hopeless addict, too long deprived of the source of her fix. He wanted her. He wanted their children. What more was there? *Love*? Cristo hadn't offered her love the last time she was with him and he likely never would. It was wiser to focus on what she could have rather than what she couldn't. Wasn't it the question she had always wanted him to ask? And did it really matter that he hadn't made an occasion of the proposal? Aside of the few gestures he had made when in initial pursuit of her, Cristo didn't have a romantic bone in his body. He was probably being practical. They were very much attracted to each other and it made sense for them to marry and share the children, she conceded ruefully, but she was slightly amazed that he was willing to surrender his freedom again after his first unhappy marriage.

'Are you sure about this?'

His sooty lashes swept up on his level gaze. 'I know what I want.'

'But is it really us as a family unit?'

'Do I get to wake up to you almost every morning?' Cristo raised a mocking brow. 'That's my sole demand. That's what I want and need.'

Erin was not quite convinced of that when two little wriggling noisy bodies tried to get into bed with them at dawn the next morning. Aghast, Cristo snatched up his boxers to make himself presentable and looked on in disbelief as the twins cuddled up between them, providing as effective a barrier as a wall.

'What are you doing in Mummy's bed?' Lorcan demanded curiously.

'Your mother and I are getting married very soon,' Cristo announced instantly.

Erin stiffened in dismay. 'Cristo, I didn't say yes.'

Cristo sent her a shocked look, his eyes dancing with wicked amusement. 'Are you saying that you took repeated gross advantage of me last night without any intention of making an honest man of me and doing the decent thing?'

Erin reddened at his mockery, the ache of her well-used body reminding her that after the enthusiasm she had demonstrated between the sheets he naturally took her agreement to marry him somewhat for granted. 'No, I'm not saying that.'

'Then I can go ahead and make the wedding arrangements?'

Erin nodded uncertainly, thoroughly shaken by the concept of becoming his bride. 'Shouldn't we have a living-together trial first?'

'Nope. You might change your mind. I refuse to be put on trial. And on a more serious note, it's time I told my parents about you and the twins. I don't want them to hear from another source,' he imparted wryly. 'I'll go and see them after breakfast.'

'They live here on the island?' Now she grasped why he had never offered to bring her to Thesos for a visit.

'They have a second home here. They use it weekends, holidays.' He shrugged. 'They're here right now.'

'How do you think they'll react?'

'I suspect my foster mother will be overjoyed—she's crazy about children.'

'Just not so crazy about me?' Erin remarked uncomfortably as the twins scampered out of bed and she followed suit.

'Some misunderstanding must've lain behind the strange impression you received of my foster mother during that phone call you made while you were pregnant. Appollonia had no reason to think badly of you. She knew nothing about you.'

The four of them enjoyed breakfast on the terrace and then Cristo left to visit his parents and Erin changed into a swimsuit, packed a bag and took the children down to the beach As the morning ticked slowly past she wondered anxiously what sort of a reception Cristo was receiving from his parents. His foster parents, she reminded herself again, having studied a picture on the wall of a glamorous young couple standing on the deck of a yacht and guessed that the glossy pair were Cristo's birth parents. When she came back from the beach, she let Jenny take the exhausted twins and went for a shower, emerging to phone her mother and describe the island and the house and, finally, their plans to marry. Her parent was very pleased by her news.

Choosing a book from the well-stocked, handsome library to entertain her until lunchtime, Erin relaxed in a cushioned lounger in the shade below the trees. She was drowsing in the heat when a slight sound alerted her to the awareness that she was no longer alone. Taking off her sunglasses, she sat up and frowned at Cristo, who looked grim. Lines of strain were indented between his nose and mouth, his black hair was tousled and stubble darkened the revealing downward curve of his beautiful mouth.

'What's up?' Erin demanded worriedly, checking her watch. He had been gone for hours. It was two in the afternoon.

As he sank down heavily opposite her Erin leant a little closer and sniffed. 'Have you been drinking?'

'I might have had a couple while I was waiting on the doctor's arrival with Vasos,' he volunteered half under his breath. 'It's been such a ghastly morning that I don't really remember.'

'Who needed a doctor?' she exclaimed.

'My mother.'

'Appollonia's taken ill?'

Cristo dealt her a troubled appraisal. 'It was her…she was the one who hired the private detective. I wouldn't have believed it if she hadn't known enough to convince me. My father is in shock—he had no idea what was going on.'

Erin was bemused. 'What are you talking about?'

'My mother hired Will Grimes.'

Her eyes widened while she recognised how much that staggering discovery had upset him. There was enormous sorrow in his unshielded eyes that made her wince and long to hold him close, for she knew how deeply attached he was to the couple who had raised him. In fact it hurt her so much to see him wounded in such a way that she stopped lying to herself in that same moment: all her proud pretences and defences fell away and she was left to face the inescapable truth that she still loved Cristophe Donakis and had never stopped loving him.

CHAPTER TEN

'APPOLLONIA learned that you and I had been together for at least a year from one of my friends. She was always ridiculously eager for me to settle down and have a family and she became convinced that you were holding me back from that development. She was obsessed with the idea of me marrying another Greek and spending more time here in Greece,' Cristo explained with a heavy sigh as he sat opposite Erin, who was studying him fixedly. 'She paid a private detective to investigate you and eventually told him that she would pay him a bonus if he would use whatever means were within his power to break us up.'

'But that's crazy,' Erin whispered, reeling from the unexpected tale he was telling her. 'You're an adult. How could your mother interfere in your life like that?'

'Appollonia seems honestly to have believed that she was doing it for the sake of my future happiness, *koukla mou*. How I might feel about it or how much damage she might do in the process to me or you never seems to have entered her head until it was too late.'

'How on earth did you realise that it was your foster mother who had hired the detective?'

'I was telling her about you and the twins and she

suddenly made a rather scornful reference to the thefts from the spa. That immediately made me suspicious because she did not get that information from me. It could only have come from the detective she hired. Once she grasped that you were the mother of my children she was very shocked and guilty and in that state she blurted out the whole story. My father, Vasos, was appalled and he asked her what she had been thinking of...'

'Did you tell her that I wasn't the thief?' Erin asked ruefully.

'Of course. She didn't ask the detective what weapons he used to bring about our split, in fact she didn't want to know the dirty details, and once it was achieved she invited Lisandra to dinner and dangled her under my nose. I told her about the doctored photos and Sally being rewarded for identifying you as the thief. I also told her that it was her fault that Lorcan and Nuala were strangers until I met them two weeks ago. She remembered your phone call. She did honestly believe that you had been stealing from me and that was how she justified her interference—you were a wicked woman and I needed help to break free of your malign influence. That had become her excuse and when that excuse was taken from her she became extremely distressed. Vasos was shouting at her and it all got very hysterical and overheated.' Cristo groaned, luxuriant black lashes almost hitting his exotic cheekbones as he briefly closed his eyes in frustration. 'In the end we called the local doctor to administer a sedative to calm her down...'

'Oh, my goodness, is this the reason she had a nervous breakdown when your marriage went wrong?'

'Yes, although none of us appreciated that at the time.

But she felt hugely guilty at having encouraged me to marry Lisandra.'

'No offence intended, Cristo, but right now Appollonia sounds like the mother-in-law from hell,' Erin remarked with an apologetic grimace.

'I think it is good that the truth has come out at last.' Cristo was seemingly determined to find a positive angle. 'Possibly Appollonia's secret arrangement with the detective has been the burden on her conscience which damaged her recovery from the breakdown she suffered. She is still a fragile personality but she wasn't always like that.'

'Was your PA got to by the detective as well? Was that why my calls were never put through and my letters were returned unread?'

Cristo sighed, 'My foster mother told her you were stalking me and that she'd be grateful if Amelia shielded me from nuisance calls and letters. Amelia probably believed she was doing me a favour.'

'Bloody hell!' Erin erupted furiously, standing up and walking away, only to spin back. 'No wonder I couldn't get hold of you!'

Cristo appraised with appreciation her slim, pale, delicately curved body in the brief red bikini she wore. 'If it's any consolation, Appollonia is the party most punished by the fallout from all this.'

Turning pink at the intensity of the gaze resting on her heaving breasts, Erin crossed her arms to interrupt his view. She hated the way he could just look at her and her body would have an involuntary reaction while her brain fogged over. 'And how do you make that out?'

'You're the one in possession of grandchildren she has never seen. Had she known you were carrying my child she would never have targeted you and she would have supported you in every way possible. I told her how alone you had been and she felt guiltier than ever,' he completed wryly.

'So, what happens now?'

'We go down to the village and see the priest and fill out the forms for our wedding.'

'You want to get married here on the island?' Erin was taken aback by the idea.

'I'll fly out your mother along with any friends you want to attend.' Seeing that that assurance had no visible effect, Cristo unfolded to his full impressive height, adding, 'We've been apart a long time—I don't want to wait long for the wedding.'

'I didn't realise it would be happening so soon,' Erin responded tentatively. 'When I agreed to come here it was only for a week to escape the press because you got so hot and bothered about them.'

A faint smile softened the harsh curve of his shapely mouth. 'Everything has changed between us since then, *koukla mou.*'

It had changed in the bedroom, Erin reflected guiltily, recalling how easily she had succumbed to his hot-blooded hunger for her. She had said yes where she should have said no and that was the only green light that a male with Cristo's high voltage libido required.

'I barely remember my birth parents. They're just a stylish photo on the wall,' Cristo remarked tautly. 'The first five years of my life I was raised by nannies. I was always being told not to *bother* my parents because they were such *busy* people. They had no time for me and little interest.'

Erin was frowning. 'Go on...'

'I didn't know what a normal home and parents were like until Vasos and Appollonia took charge of me. They spent time with me, talked to me, took an interest in my small achievements and gave me love. I owe everything I am today to them. I want to do the same thing for Lorcan and Nuala.'

She had not realised that his early years had been so bleak and she understood his attitude, for her own childhood had been almost as troubled and insecure. Marrying Cristo made sense, she reasoned ruefully. She wanted her children to have a full-time father and the chance of a happy family life. Cristo was offering her that option and she put as high a value on that lifestyle as he apparently did. But he would not have wanted to marry her had she not had the twins and that hurt. It hurt that he didn't love and want her with the same intensity that he wanted their children.

That evening Sam Morton phoned her. 'Your mother told me you were in Greece. I was shocked.'

'We're getting married, Sam.'

'Yes, she told me that as well. Of course that's the safest choice for Donakis if he wants access to his children. I understand that he consulted an expert in family law in London to find out exactly where he stood. Watch your step, Erin. In a Greek court, he could gain custody of the kids.'

Erin's blood ran cold at that forecast. 'Are you trying to scare me? We're getting married, not divorced.'

'I think it's very convenient for Donakis to marry you now but he wasn't interested in marrying you three years ago. Don't forget that.'

Sadly that was a fact that Erin never forgot and she

could have done without the second opinion. Had Cristo consulted a legal expert? How had Sam found that out? No doubt someone knew someone in the legal field who also knew Sam and word had got back to him in that way. Ought she to be worried? She supposed it was understandable that Cristo should have sought advice when he first found out that he was a father. That was not in itself wrong. Even so, the knowledge sent a little buzz of insecurity through her that she could not shake.

'Cristo,' she said towards the end of the evening while she worried about whether it was foolish of her to trust Cristo to such an extent. 'Would you mind very much if I slept on my own until the wedding?'

Cristo frowned. 'Not if it's important to you.'

'With Mum arriving a few days before the wedding, it would really be more comfortable for me,' she told him stiffly.

One week later, Cristo and Erin were married in the little church overlooking the town harbour. She wore a white lace dress, tight on the arms and fitted to make the most of her slender figure, obtained from a designer in Athens. Her mother had thought her daughter was being controversial buying into the whole white wedding fantasy when she already had two young children but Erin had seen no reason why her special day should not live up to her girlhood dreams. After all, she loved Cristo Donakis and preferred to be optimistic about their future.

The Greek Orthodox service presided over by the bearded priest in his long dark robe was traditional and meaningful. The church was crammed with well-wishers and filled with flowers. The scent of incense and the fresh-orange-blossom circlet placed on her head mingled headily and, strange as it all was to her, she loved it, loved Cristo's hand in hers, the steadiness of his lion-gold gaze and utter lack of nerves. For the first time she felt that they were meant to be together and she fought off downbeat thoughts about what his wedding to Lisandra might have been like as it was clearly not on his mind.

The days running up to their wedding had been exceptionally busy. She had had to take Nuala to an Athens hospital to have her cast checked. Mercifully everything had been in order and the little girl had not required a replacement. That appointment had been followed by a shopping trip to buy Erin's wedding gown. The next day she had first made the acquaintance of Cristo's father, Vasos Denes, when he came over to meet the twins. Initially appearing stern and quiet, Vasos had slowly shaken off his discomfiture over his wife's interference in Cristo's private life and its disastrous side effects to relax in his son's home and Erin had decided that he was a lovely man. She had been surprised when Cristo explained that his father's company was on the edge of bankruptcy but that the older man refused to accept his financial help. She had soon grasped from whom Cristo had learned his principles and even if his volatile nature warred against them and occasionally won—as in when he had blackmailed her into going to Italy with him—she knew Cristo did try to respect scruples and operate accordingly.

In a gesture made purely for Cristo and his foster father's sake, Erin had volunteered to take the children to visit Appollonia Denes at their villa on the outskirts of the town. Even on the medication her doctor had advised to help her with her low mood, the older woman had been stunned to see the twins and tears had trailed slowly down her cheeks while she attempted awkwardly to express her regret for the actions she had taken almost three years earlier. That she absolutely adored Cristo had shone out of her and her wondering delight in Lorcan and Nuala had inspired pity in Erin. She knew it would take time before she could forgive Appollonia for what she had done but she was willing to make the effort.

Cristo had thrown himself into spending every afternoon with the twins. Watching her children respond to his interest, noting the shocking similarity in their lively demanding personalities, Erin had known that marrying Cristo was the right step to take. Lorcan was already learning that when his father said no he meant it and Nuala's tantrums had become less frequent. The first time she condescended to call Cristo, 'Daddy', he admitted to Erin that he felt as if he had won the lottery.

Her mother had travelled to Thesos in the company of Tom and Melissa. Sam had turned down his invitation but had sent a lavish present. The day before the wedding, Cristo had taken them all out sailing. He was a wonderful host and had been in the very best of moods. Erin had taken that as a compliment: Cristo was happy that they were getting married. And she had during the week that had passed learned to regret her request that they sleep apart until the ceremony. Intimacy brought a special closeness to their relationship and she missed it, disliking the new distance that her demand had wrought in Cristo. He was too careful to give her space. A couple of times she had lain awake into the early hours, her body taut with frustration and longing, trying to sum-

mon up the courage to go and join Cristo in the opulent master suite at the top of the stairs. Why was she
still punishing herself for wanting him? Why had she
let Sam's sour suspicious comments make her doubt
Cristo's sincerity?

Cristo lifted her hand in the car on the way back to
the house from the church and touched the shiny new
platinum ring on her finger with approval. 'Now you're
mine.'

'That sounds exceedingly caveman-type basic,' Erin
remarked.

'I suppose carrying you upstairs *before* we entertain
our guests would be even more basic?' Cristo rested
scorching golden eyes on her face as she turned fire-
engine red with sexual awareness and embarrassment.

'You're scaring me because I know you're capable of
behaving like that,' she admitted ruefully.

'I was pure caveman when I blackmailed you into
meeting me in Italy,' Cristo conceded with a sardonic
laugh. 'I do crazy things with you that I've never done
with any other woman. Italy was supposed to be an exorcism—'

Erin gave him a blank look while trying not to picture how wickedly exciting it would be if Cristo was
were to trail her straight off to his bedroom. That was
the real problem. He might be pure caveman but on
some level she liked that side of him and responded to it.
There was something uniquely satisfying about knowing she was such an object of desire to him.

'An exorcism?' she repeated.

'I couldn't stop thinking about you and how incred-
ible we were in bed. It infuriated me. I thought that if I
saw you again, slept with you again I'd be disappointed

and I could get you out of my system. My, didn't that work well?' he said with rich self-mockery. 'Here we are just three weeks later and we're married!'

'Did you and Lisandra get married in the same church?' Erin asked, no longer able to stifle her curiosity.

'Of course not. We had a massive society wedding staged in Athens. Lisandra likes to make a big splash in public.'

'But the church here and the simple service were lovely,' Erin commented softly.

His handsome mouth twisted. 'You and Lisandra are very different.'

Did he have regrets? A little ache set in somewhere in the region of Erin's heart. Erin had seen photos of his ex-wife in glossy magazines and Lisandra was much more sophisticated than she was. Most people would reckon that Cristo had married 'down' in choosing Erin and when they realised that the twins were his they would put another construction altogether on their marriage. Did that matter to her? Was she too sensitive? Expediency, rather than love, made the world go round. She didn't *need* him to love her. Evidently she didn't have that essential spark that would inspire such feelings in him or he would have fallen in love with her when they were first together and everything was all shiny and new.

'Visiting my mother in spite of what she did, allowing her to be present today and treating her like one of the family,' Cristo specified wryly. 'Lisandra would never have forgiven her.'

'I haven't forgiven Appollonia either.'

'But you're willing to *try*. I'm very grateful for that,'

Cristo told her quietly. 'You had the opportunity to get your own back by excluding her from our lives but you didn't take it. That was generous of you.'

'She truly regrets what she did. We all make mistakes.'

Cristo grasped her hand, curved lean fingers to the side of her face and brought his mouth down on hers with a hungry urgency that sent pure energy winging through her trembling body. 'I'm wrecking your make-up,' he groaned against her sultry mouth.

'Doesn't matter,' Erin proclaimed breathlessly, looking up at him with starry eyes and a thundering heartbeat.

Cristo handed her a tissue for the lipstick he had smeared. 'Our guests await us but first…I have a gift for you.'

He handed her a tiny jewellery box, which she flipped open. It contained a band of diamonds, an eternity ring. 'Cristo, it's beautiful but I haven't got you anything.'

'My gift is having you back in my bed again,' he murmured lazily.

The burning intensity of the look that accompanied that statement was like a blowtorch. She tottered out of the car on wobbling knees, struggling to pin a social smile to her lips. He really *really* wanted her and that was good, a healthy sign for a very practical marriage, she told herself earnestly, striving hard to be sensible while she admired the new rings sparkling on her finger. Cristo for eternity would be paradise, she thought dizzily, barely able to credit that he was finally hers. She watched as the twins ran to him and he scooped them up in both arms in a movement that made Lorcan and Nuala break into fits of laughter.

'He's so good with them,' her mother remarked approvingly from the front door that stood open. 'I expect you're planning on more children.'

'Not at the minute,' Erin told her mother frankly. 'I think we'll be getting used to being married for quite a while.'

'Cristo looks happier and more relaxed than I've seen him in years,' Vasos commented approvingly at her elbow. 'You're good for each other. I only wish that my wife's interference hadn't parted you when you should have stayed together.'

'It's water under the bridge now,' Erin said lightly as she looked up at the older man.

'I had an argument with my son when he said he couldn't possibly take a honeymoon while my company was failing. Don't worry,' Vasos urged comfortably. 'I soon talked sense into him. Of course you're having a honeymoon.'

Erin swallowed uncomfortably. She knew how hard Cristo had worked in his efforts to support his father's business, which had suffered badly in the difficult economic climate in Greece, but she also knew that Vasos' stubborn independent streak had made it an almost impossible challenge. 'He worries a lot about you.'

'He'll get over it,' Vasos replied staunchly.

'No, he won't actually,' she told him in a low voice. 'He'll feel like the worst failure if your business goes down. Why won't you let Cristo help you?'

'I could never accept money from Cristo.'

'But you're his family.'

'When he came to us as a child he was a fantastically rich little boy and I swore never to take advantage of that.'

'Times change. For a start, he's an adult, not a child any more. He loves you very much. Isn't it selfish to force him to stand by and do nothing while you go bankrupt? He'll be devastated.'

Vasos frowned.

'Please don't be offended with me,' Erin begged. 'I just wanted you to know what it's like for him not to be allowed to help when you're in trouble. In the same situation wouldn't you want to help him no matter what?'

'I will consider that angle,' Vasos replied after a long minute of silence, his stern face troubled. 'You can be very blunt, Erin…but you do understand Cristo.'

'Hopefully.' With a warm smile, Erin moved away to greet other guests, praying she hadn't said too much to Cristo's foster father. Cristo would probably be furious if he knew she had said anything, but negotiations between him and the older man were currently at a standstill and she had decided that she might as well speak up on Cristo's behalf.

Late afternoon, Cristo informed her that they were leaving. 'To go where?' she pressed.

'It's a surprise.'

'I haven't even packed—'

'There's no need. A new wardrobe awaits you at our destination. You don't need to worry about the twins either because your mother has agreed to stay on here until we return. Let's go—'

'Like…*right now*?' Erin exclaimed. 'I need to get changed—'

'No. I want to be the one to take off that dress,' Cristo confessed, gazing down into her eyes with a sensual look of anticipation that sparked fire in her bloodstream.

They flew to the airport in the helicopter and, having

presented their passports, boarded the jet straight away. By then, having been up at the crack of dawn, Erin was smothering yawns and the drone of the engines sent her into a sound sleep. When she wakened, she was embarrassed by the poor showing she was making as a bride and barely had time to tidy her mussed hair and repair her make-up before they landed.

'You've brought me back to Italy,' she registered in surprise, recognising the airport. 'Why Italy?'

'It's where we began again even if we didn't appreciate it that weekend.'

And alighting from the limo that brought them to the villa and struggling to walk in the high-heeled sandals that were now pinching horribly, she decided that he had made a good point. Her emotions had rekindled along with her desire for him. It had been time out of time and wonderful in the strangest way of happiness coming when you least expected it to do so.

'I gave the housekeeper the weekend off.'

Cristo swept her up in his arms to carry her through the door he had unlocked.

It was a romantic gesture she hadn't expected from him and, eyes widening, she smiled up at him, colliding with dark golden eyes that made her heart race. They walked up the stairs, though, hand in hand and she almost giggled, unfamiliar as she was with such signs from Cristo, who was usually cooler than cool in that department. In the bedroom doorway she stilled, scanning the room, which had been transformed with lush arrangements of white flowers and dozens of candles with little flames that leapt and glowed in the darkness: she was transfixed.

'Good heavens,' she murmured, totally stunned by the display. 'You organised this?'

'I wanted it to be perfect for you.'

Hugely impressed, Erin smiled again and walked on in, kicking off her tight shoes with a sigh of relief.

'Now you've shrunk,' Cristo teased, uncorking the bottle of champagne awaiting them and handing her an elegant flute bubbling with the pale golden liquid.

Erin sipped. 'Did you do something like this for Lisandra?'

He frowned. 'Why do you keep on asking about her?'

'Well, *did* you?' Erin persisted.

'No, I didn't. It wasn't that kind of marriage. I thought you would have worked out by now that I married Lisandra on the rebound,' Cristo imparted with a rueful twist of his mouth. 'I reeled away from the wreckage of our relationship and made the biggest mistake of all.'

On the rebound? She liked that news. She liked it even better that he was willing to admit that his first marriage had been a mistake. It soothed the hurt place inside her that had formed when she had realised he had taken a wife within months of their split. An extraordinary urge to move closer and hug him also assailed Erin. She might want to wrap that confession in fairy lights and laugh and smile over it but an aching sadness afflicted her at the same time. Three years back, he must have cared about her more than she had realised but she had still lost him through no fault of her own.

'You weren't in love with your wife?' she prompted stiffly.

'I thought I'd made that clear.'

'Why did you marry her, then?'

'After losing faith in you I had no heart for dating.

My marriage pleased my family, gave me something to focus on other than you, but it was a catastrophe.' Cristo shifted a broad shoulder in a fatalistic shrug and gave her a wry look. 'This is our wedding night. I don't want to talk about this now.'

Something to focus on other than you. And suddenly Erin understood something that she had never quite believed in before. When they broke up, he had been badly hurt too, he had suffered as well. He had rushed into a marriage that he had hoped would cure him of his unhappiness. But now she was suddenly reflecting on the eternity ring and the beautiful bower of flowers and candles he had had prepared for their arrival and her heart swelled with warmth and forgiveness. He was doing things he had never done before. He was trying to show her that he had feelings for her and naturally he didn't want her rabbiting on about Lisandra in the middle of it.

'I love you,' he told her in a roughened undertone, detaching the champagne glass from her nerveless fingers and setting it aside so that he could pull her close. His eyes were bright with emotion in the flickering candlelight. 'I was in love with you when we broke up but I didn't know it. You've haunted me ever since. When I saw you in that photo with Sam and his staff, all I could think about was seeing you again. I lied to myself. I told myself that it was only sex and that I wanted to get over the memory of you, but I was still in love with you when I brought you here that weekend. When I woke up beside you the next morning I knew I didn't ever want to let you go again.'

Tears welled up in Erin's amethyst eyes and any strand of lingering resentment over that weekend vanished, for they had found each other again in this peaceful house, re-establishing the connection they had forged years earlier. That he loved her meant so much that she could barely contain the huge surge of happiness spreading inside her. 'We've lost so much time when we could have been together,' she sighed.

'But we're still young enough to make up for that and maybe while we were apart we both learned stuff we needed to know,' Cristo countered more thoughtfully. 'But if we had stayed together I would have eventually married you. I just wasn't in a hurry.'

'And this time around you probably felt like you didn't have a choice,' Erin completed.

Cristo spun her round to run down the zip on her gown. 'No, I thought very carefully about that decision. I didn't have to live with you to play a part in the twins' lives and my financial support would have taken care of any problems you had. No, I asked you to marry me because I wanted *you* in my life every day.'

Smiling widely at that assurance, a glow of pleasure lighting up her eyes, Erin turned back to help him out of his jacket. 'And there I was thinking that you had only married me because you thought it was the *practical* thing to do!'

Cristo curved long fingers to her cheekbones and groaned. 'I know it was a useless proposal. I should never have asked you when we were in bed but I couldn't hold back any longer. Wives are a lot harder to lose than girlfriends and I needed to know that you were mine again for ever, *pethi mou*.'

'I like the sound of for ever,' Erin savoured, shimmying out of her lace gown and standing in her frivolous silk and lace bra and panties, a blue garter adorning one slim stocking-clad thigh.

'I like the underpinnings,' Cristo teased, fiery dark eyes welded to her scantily clad figure as he appraised her with lingering intensity. 'But I'll like you out of them even better and after a week of celibacy it's over-kill.'

'Is it?' Her brows lifted, her uncertainty visible.

Laughing, Cristo picked her up and dropped her down on the gloriously comfortable bed. 'You look gorgeous but I did notice that the separate bedrooms made your mother more comfortable in our home, *latria mou*.'

'I wanted tonight to be special,' Erin whispered, running a possessive hand up a shirt-clad arm.

He sat up and discarded his shirt with alacrity, revealing a hard brown torso taut and roped with muscle. She spread her fingers there instead, revelling in the solid reassuring beat of his heart. 'I forgot to tell you that I loved you.'

'And as punishment you have to tell me at least ten times every day,' Cristo delivered, lowering his head to claim a long passionate kiss that sent her hands up to clasp his head. 'You know, I thought it might take you much longer to forgive me for not being there when you needed me…and even worse marrying another woman.'

Erin smiled. 'No, I know you've been through tough times too. What I didn't understand is why you were suddenly doing all the romantic stuff you never did before. Do you remember what our first ever row was about?'

'I forgot Valentine's Day once we were dating. Well, actually I didn't. I'd always avoided the mushy stuff as it raises unfair expectations and I was embarrassed about the one I sent you before you agreed to go out with me.'

'A card?' Erin scorned. 'A *card* would rouse expectations?'

Cristo winced. 'I thought that sort of thing, like meeting each other's families, should be kept for someone you're serious about. We had only been together eleven months and twenty three days…'

Her eyes widened. 'You counted how long we were together?'

'I was always a maths whizz,' Cristo fielded deadpan.

Erin was impressed. She glanced around her candlelit flower-bedecked bower and smiled happily at what that display said: she had finally made the grade for the mushy stuff! He would never ignore Valentine's Day again. She gazed up at him, enthralled by his lean, darkly handsome features and the tender look in his beautiful dark eyes.

'I missed you *so* much!' he breathed suddenly. 'Something would remind me and then, boom, all these images would flood my head. And then I would remember what I thought you had done and get really angry that I was thinking about you again.'

Erin reached up and kissed him. 'That time is gone. Now we've got something better and stronger, something that will last—'

'For ever,' he slotted in with determination.

Her eyes slid shut as he claimed her parted lips in another hungry, demanding kiss. Heat spread inside her with tingling, burning energy and she gave herself up to desire and happiness without any sense of fear at all.

* * *

Two years later, Erin hosted the grand opening of Cristo's first spa hotel on Thesos. Built beside a secluded beach and surrounded by lush pine forest, it provided a back-to-nature retreat with luxury on tap for the discerning traveller, and as the latest must-have place to go it was already fully booked six months in advance. As Cristo had been held up, Vasos and Appollonia Denes were by her side.

A sea change had taken place in her relationship with the older couple. The passage of time had soothed the bad memories of the past and Erin's natural resentment. Appollonia had grown stronger and calmer and as she recovered from her excessive nervousness and fatal tendency to apologise for everything had confided that her greatest fear had always been that Cristo would discover what she had done and refuse to forgive her. Once the secret was out, Appollonia had had to deal with her guilt, and forging a healthy, normal relationship with Erin and the twins had gone a long way to achieving that.

Vasos had ultimately accepted a loan from Cristo to save his business but had insisted that Cristo accept a partnership in the firm, an arrangement that had left both men with their pride and principles intact. Cristo had been overjoyed that Erin's intervention had wrought a change in his foster father's stubborn outlook.

For the first year of her marriage Erin had spent a great deal of time checking out the spa facilities in her husband's hotel empire and travelling a great deal. Jenny and the twins had often accompanied her while her mother was a frequent visitor to Thesos. During the second year Erin had begun supervising the final touches to the new island spa, which was providing much needed work for the locals and had already prompted the opening of several tourist-type businesses in the village.

Sheathed in a shimmering silver evening gown, she posed for photographers and waved back as Sam and his former secretary, Janice, raised their glasses to salute her from across the room. Sam Morton was about to embark on a worldwide cruise with his recently acquired bride. Erin smiled warmly at the other couple, currently engaged in chatting to her mother, Deidre, thinking that she had been blind not to appreciate that Janice cared about Sam and that her removal from the scene would make it easier for Sam to see Janice in a different light. Sam had had to retire before he could appreciate how much he missed Janice's company and a friendly dinner date to catch up on news had eventually resulted in his second marriage.

'You look amazing, Mrs Donakis,' a rich dark drawl purred above her head as a possessive hand curved to her hip.

Erin whirled round. 'Cristo, when did you get back?'

'Half an hour ago. I had the quickest shower and change on record,' he confided. 'That's it, though. I won't be off on another trip for at least six weeks.'

Erin feasted her eyes on her handsome husband. He looked spectacular in his dark designer suit. The female photographer was watching him as though dinner had just walked through the door, but Erin was accustomed to the buzz that Cristo brought to the women in a room and it didn't bother her. Jenny came through the door with Lorcan and Nuala. Nuala, adorable in a fancy party dress, skipped over to show it off to her father, little hands holding out the skirt as if she were about to perform a curtsy.

Lorcan took his hands out of his pockets at his father's request and then ran off to try and climb the huge palm tree in the centre of the foyer.

'Lorcan!' Cristo yelled, and he strode over to lift his squirming son off the trunk and imprisoned him under one arm, talking to the little boy before setting him down again.

'Lorcan's such a boy,' Nuala pronounced, rolling her eyes with pained superiority.

Erin's mother held out her hands to the children and they latched onto her immediately, begging her to take them down to the beach.

'I wonder what the third one will be like,' Cristo commented, his dark golden gaze dipping briefly to the barely perceptible bump visible below Erin's dress.

'A mix of our genes, some good, some bad.'

'I can't wait to see our baby,' Cristo confessed.

A warm sense of tenderness filled Erin, and only their public location stopped her leaning in to hug him. She hadn't initially been sure about how another child would fit into their busy lives, but one of the main reasons she'd come round to the idea had been the awareness that Cristo had missed out on the experience of the twins as babies. While she had conceived faster than she had expected, she had thoroughly enjoyed having a supportive, interested male by her side to share every development in her pregnancy and the sight of Cristo with tears in his eyes when he saw the first scan of their child was one she would never forget.

The evening wore on in chats with influential people and business associates. The twins were whisked home to bed and Cristo, his attention consistently returning to his wife's lovely face and smile, was unashamedly relieved when they could finally take their leave of their guests.

'I hate being away from you now,' he confided, lifting her out of the four-wheel drive he had taken her home in.

'You're not away half as much as you used to be.'

'I can do a lot of my work at home.' At the foot of the stairs he swung her up in his arms and insisted on carrying her the rest of the way in spite of her protests. 'I know your feet are killing you, *latria mou*.'

She kicked her shoes off when he put her down, holding up the skirt of her gown so that she didn't trip on the trailing hem. 'But the shoes did look gorgeous,' she pointed out.

Cristo framed her laughing face with tender hands. 'You don't need to suffer to look beautiful.'

'Only a man could say that. I still can't believe that you were *born* with eyebrows that stay in shape,' Erin lamented. 'It's so unfair.'

'I would love you even without all the waxing,' Cristo intoned huskily.

Erin tried to imagine getting into bed with a pair of hairy legs and barely repressed a shudder. 'The things you say.'

'I'm trying to impress you with how crazy I am about you.' Cristo sighed with a long-suffering look belied by the amusement dancing in his dark golden eyes. 'It's an uphill challenge.'

'No, it's not. I love you too, naturally perfect brows included,' his wife informed him, gazing up at him with an appreciation she couldn't hide. *Mine*, every natural instinct said and she adored the fact.

He bent his handsome dark head and kissed her softly

with all the skill at his disposal, and her head swam and her knees wobbled and the glory of loving Cristo swept over her like a consuming tide, filled with happiness and acceptance and pure joy.

* * * * *

A sneaky peek at next month...

MODERN™

INTERNATIONAL AFFAIRS, SEDUCTION & PASSION GUARANTEED

My wish list for next month's titles...

In stores from 20th July 2012:

❑ Contract with Consequences – Miranda Lee

❑ The Man She Shouldn't Crave – Lucy Ellis

❑ A Tainted Beauty – Sharon Kendrick

❑ The Dangerous Jacob Wilde – Sandra Marton

In stores from 3rd August 2012:

❑ The Sheikh's Last Gamble – Trish Morey

❑ The Girl He'd Overlooked – Cathy Williams

❑ One Night With The Enemy – Abby Green

❑ His Last Chance at Redemption – Michelle Conder

❑ The Hidden Heart of Rico Rossi – Kate Hardy

Available at WHSmith, Tesco, Asda, Eason, Amazon and Apple

Just can't wait?

Special Offers

Every month we put together collections and longer reads written by your favourite authors.

Here are some of next month's highlights— and don't miss our fabulous discount online!

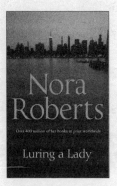

On sale 3rd August

On sale 3rd August

On sale 3rd August

Save 20% on all Special Releases

Find out more at
www.millsandboon.co.uk/specialreleases

Visit us Online

MILLS & BOON Book Club

2 Free Books!

Join the Mills & Boon Book Club

Want to read more **Modern**™ books? We're offering you **2 more** absolutely **FREE!**

We'll also treat you to these fabulous extras:

 Books up to 2 months ahead of shops

 FREE home delivery

 Bonus books with our special rewards scheme

 Exclusive offers and much more!

Get your free books now!

 Visit us Online

Find out more at
www.millsandboon.co.uk/freebookoffer

SUBS/ONLINE/M